MACGREGOR'S COVE

Running the Bell Inn, which sits high above Macgregor's Cove, is a busy yet peaceful life for Amaryllis's family — but their lodger Kit Chesterton arrives with a heavy secret in tow, which threatens to disturb the quiet waters. Meanwhile, a recent influx in contraband starts ripples of suspicion about smugglers, and Amaryllis's sister sets her sights on Adam Whitlock, who has recently returned from India with a shady companion. Despite the sinister events washing through the Cove, love surfaces as friendship becomes romance and strangers become family.

JUNE DAVIES

◆

MACGREGOR'S COVE

Complete and Unabridged

LINFORD
Leicester

First published in Great Britain in 2018

First Linford Edition
published 2020

*A catalogue record for this book is available
from the British Library.*

ISBN 978–1–4448–4484–9

Published by
Ulverscroft Limited
Anstey, Leicestershire

Set by Words & Graphics Ltd.
Anstey, Leicestershire
Printed and bound in Great Britain by
T. J. International Ltd., Padstow, Cornwall

This book is printed on acid-free paper

1

When Amaryllis Macgregor was a little girl, her first chore every morning was polishing the stout brass bell which gave the cliff-top inn overlooking Macgregor's Cove its name.

This daily task at The Bell had long since been taken up by her younger sister, Betsy, and Amaryllis's first job upon *this* hot, misty summer morning had been setting off from the inn-house hours before breakfast to gather soft fruit from the St. Agnes ruins.

The medieval priory's once carefully-tended orchards and gardens had long since grown wild and, like much of the land along this expanse of Lancashire coastline, the St. Agnes ruins were the property of Elias Whitlock from Haddonsell Grange. Mr Whitlock hadn't minded the Macgregors gathering the old priory's fruit,

1

but Amaryllis couldn't help wonder whether this privilege was about to change now young Mr Adam was returning from India to manage the Haddonsell estate.

When her willow trugs were brimming with strawberries, gooseberries, blackcurrants and the first sweet cherries of the season, Amaryllis started homewards. Presently, the dunes gave way to caves and green cliffs, Uncle Iain Macgregor's little boatyard slipped into view and a distance beyond, perched high on the cliff-top like a nesting great grey gull, stood Amaryllis's home, The Bell Inn.

She could see her young sister now. Betsy was standing on tiptoe upon a three-legged stool, rubbing the brass bell vigorously. As Amaryllis drew closer, she saw Betsy closing her eyes and murmuring the traditional hope — the *prayer* — that the bell might not ring out this day, for it was a tolling bell, rung only upon sight or sound of a vessel in distress.

As usual, Flossie was curled up with her head on her paws beside her beloved Betsy. Child and dog were seldom parted, and since Betsy lost her hearing during a serious illness several years ago, Amaryllis believed Flossie somehow had become the little girl's ears. Now, the silky white dog stirred at Amaryllis's approach. Wagging her plumy tail, she went to Betsy's side, snuffling at the little girl's hand.

Betsy looked around, spotted Amaryllis and waved, her rosy face wreathed in smiles.

'Did you get everything on Ma's list?' she called, racing across the cobbled yard.

'I did!' laughed Amaryllis, lowering the trugs so Betsy — and Flossie — might peek inside. 'And more besides!'

'Cherries!' exclaimed Betsy, whose lip-reading of those she knew well was almost word-perfect, and often accurate enough with less familiar folk so she could follow, or at least gain the gist of, a question or conversation. 'Cherry pie is Pa's favourite!'

'There weren't many ripe for picking, so I had to shin up several trees to gather enough for a pie — I tore my dress *and* grazed my knee climbing down,' she went on, suddenly aware her light brown hair had escaped its braid and was straggling loose. 'I'd best get tidied up before Ma sees me!'

Amaryllis sped across to the innhouse, which adjoined the inn at such a curious angle the Macgregor family's home looked out across the sea from three of its sides. She was scurrying around to the kitchen door when her elder sister Dorcas swept out through the front porch, a gossamer-light lemon shawl swirling about her shoulders and a becoming bonnet shading her fair complexion.

'Why has it taken you such a time to gather a few baskets of fruit?' she exclaimed. 'Ma's waiting for you to peel potatoes — you know fine well how many folk are arriving at the inn today!'

'I thought *you* were helping Ma in the big kitchen while I went to the ruins!' exclaimed Amaryllis, vexed. 'Where on earth are you going?'

'Into town. I need ribbons for my lilac dress — it looks shabby beyond words!' Dorcas shook her head, her glowing red-gold curls bobbing around the frilled edge of her bonnet. 'I'll be singing tomorrow evening, and I can't possibly wear my lilac dress without doing *something* to adorn it!'

'You're going into St. Agnes to buy ribbons when we've a mountain of chores to do?' challenged Amaryllis in disbelief. 'Tomorrow is a sing-song with Uncle Iain and Great Aunt Macgregor — not one of the Whitlocks' fancy balls at Haddonsell Grange!'

'It doesn't matter how trivial the occasion,' retorted Dorcas aloofly. 'A young lady must *always* be mindful of her appearance.'

She cast a disparaging glance at her sister's dishevelled hair and damp, sand-spattered skirts. 'You'll never

5

catch a wealthy husband and make a good marriage, Am.'

'I'm not certain I *want* to catch a husband — wealthy or otherwise!' retorted Amaryllis mutinously.

'Then you're a fool, Amaryllis Macgregor!' returned Dorcas airily. 'A woman without a husband has no status whatsoever! You'll probably end up a miserable old maid like Penelope Whitlock at the Grange.'

'That's a mean thing to say, Dorcas! Miss Whitlock is such a kindly person!'

'Penelope Whitlock is long past thirty with all hope of marriage gone.' Dorcas took a final, scathing appraisal of her sister. 'If Ma sees you looking like that, she *won't* be pleased!'

With that, Dorcas Macgregor flounced away along the lane towards the prosperous market town of St. Agnes.

★   ★   ★

Setting the day's batch of loaves to cool, Ethel Macgregor watched Dorcas setting off for St. Agnes from the back window of The Bell's big kitchen, and felt a familiar surge of love and pride swelling her heart.

Dorcas was a true beauty, with poise and grace to everything she did — why, even her jaunty walk had an elegant air about it!

Goodness alone knew where that girl got her looks and her dainty ways. For even on her best day, Ethel owned she'd been plain as a pikestaff and from what she'd seen of the Macgregors, Sandy's kin were no oil paintings either!

Her and Sandy weren't young when they'd wed. Ethel had feared it might be too late for babies, but although the first two came along quick enough, both were girls. Ethel hadn't borne the son she'd been praying for. There were no more babies for a very long time, and Ethel was nearly forty-four when she delivered her final child — another girl.

To give him his due, Sandy had never once blamed her for not bearing him a son — he loved his three daughters dearly and there never was a better father — but Ethel *knew* it must grieve him sorely! For wasn't it only natural for a man to want a son to bear his name and carry on the family name?

Yes, in her long and contented marriage, Ethel had but that *one* regret . . .

Kit Chesterton placed the posy of white flowers onto his parents' resting place and straightened up; his large dark eyes were sad but a wistful smile touched his lips.

'I'm thankful I was able to come home to Jamaica and spend these last months with Mama,' he reflected, turning from the graveside and looking to his older brother Geoffrey, sister-in-law Susan and Tabitha Warburton, who'd been Mama's maid, his and Geoff's nurse, and part of the Chesterton family for as long as Kit could remember.

'Even after so many years, it grieves me I wasn't here when Papa died — I never had the chance to say goodbye, or tell him . . . '

Kit's words faded, and only the songs of birds and the whispering of a hot, dry breeze stirred the silence of the leafy churchyard. His gaze returned to the headstone; Thomas Chesterton's inscription was worn and weathered now, a stark contrast to the sharp, freshly chiselled lettering of Clara's name.

'Your mama was delighted when you wrote saying you'd finished building one of your canals and were coming for a visit,' murmured Tabitha, when the little party was strolling from the churchyard. 'These past months were *very* happy for her!'

'Happy for me, too, Tabby,' he responded softly. 'It's good to be home again.'

'Do you still think of Jamaica as home?' queried his sister-in-law. 'Isn't *England* your home now?'

'My work is there, but nothing else,' replied Kit, drawing a healing breath as

9

they entered the lush, fragrant gardens of the Chestertons' villa where he'd grown up. 'Jamaica will *always* be home.'

★ ★ ★

The brothers postponed sorting through their mother's belongings until, with Kit's sailing for England on the morrow, they could delay the poignant task no longer.

They were seated on the villa's verandah in the cool of evening, their mother's little cherry-wood keepsake chest open before them. It was here Clara had stored her most personal possessions and those holding very special memories — all of her 'treasures'.

Geoffrey was glancing through a bundle of letters written in sprawling, immature hands. 'Mama must've kept every letter you and I wrote from boarding school — ' He noticed Kit opening a small package wrapped in muslin and secured with broad velvet ribbon. '*That* looks far more interesting!'

From the folds of fabric fell a small medallion, crudely fashioned from wood and carved to depict St. Christopher.

Kit turned the medallion over on his palm. The necklet was a simple strand of fine cord. It showed signs of having been worn, but it wasn't something he'd noticed their mother wearing.

'I've never seen this before.' He offered it to his brother. 'Have you?'

'No, and I can't imagine Mama ever wearing such a poorly-made trinket,' shrugged Geoffrey, with an affectionate grin. 'Perhaps she kept it because *your* given name is Christopher — you know how sentimental Mama could be!'

He indicated several scraps of coarse paper that had also slipped from the muslin. 'What are *they*?'

'Some old letters,' replied Kit, a perplexed frown creasing his forehead as he leafed through the tattered pages.

11

'But these letters aren't written to our mother, Geoff — they're addressed to somebody named *Marietta!*

'Why on earth would Mama have another woman's letters?' He passed them across the table to Geoffrey.

'These are love letters!' exclaimed Geoffrey, glancing over the uneven lines of faded black ink. 'Sent to this Marietta woman from an Englishman called Alexander! The name means nothing to me.' He handed back the letters. 'And from the sound of it, I very much doubt he was likely to have been a friend — or even a passing acquaintance — of *our* family!'

'I don't recognise either of their names,' remarked Kit, scanning the pages more carefully. 'Ah, this Alexander chap wasn't resident here! He writes about *returning* to Jamaica — and marrying Marietta.'

'It doesn't make any sense,' opined Geoffrey with an impatient shake of his head. 'What significance could someone else's dog-eared love letters and a cheap medallion possibly have for our mother?'

Kit was no longer listening. Raising his eyes from the spidery black writing, he slid a page across the table toward Geoffrey.

'Alexander and Marietta had a son — an infant, named Christopher.' Kit swallowed hard, his thoughts racing in a score of diverse directions. '*Christopher* isn't a common name in Jamaica, is it?'

'Oh, no, Kit!' exclaimed Geoffrey in disbelief. 'That's preposterous! You're surely never thinking — '

'I don't know *what* I'm thinking,' interrupted Kit soberly. 'Look at the dates on these letters, Geoff. They were written in the year I was born! Two boys born in the same year and both named Christopher is quite a coincidence, wouldn't you say?'

'And *why* would Mama keep these things in the cherry-wood chest with her most cherished belongings,' he murmured, carefully gathering up the pages and the St. Christopher, 'unless

Marietta's old letters and this little medallion were somehow very important to her?'

★   ★   ★

Amaryllis carried a mug of cool milk from the inn-house's neat little kitchen into the sitting-room, where Betsy was engrossed in the lessons Great Aunt Mathilda Macgregor regularly set for her.

'What are you drawing?' smiled Amaryllis, setting down the milk.

'A map. Great Aunt Macgregor's been telling me how our family sailed down the Scottish coast bound for the Isle of Man, but during bad weather their boat put in here at the cove,' explained Betsy enthusiastically. 'I've been following their journey on a big map Great Aunt lent me from her bookshop, and now I'm drawing one for us to hang up in our room!'

'I've heard Great Aunt's old stories about the Macgregors, but I've never

14

actually seen where they came from,' responded Amaryllis, studying the map. 'Betsy — will you show me all this later? I have to go through to the inn and make ready the rooms before Noah brings in the packet.

'When that's done and I've given Ma a hand in the big kitchen, I've *Dorcas*'s chores to do,' she went on, mentally running through the list of jobs as she hurried from the sitting-room. 'Our sister has suddenly decided we need more honey — and taken herself off to Haddonsell Grange for six more pots!'

'Is Dorcas setting her cap at the young master, Ammie?'

The question stopped Amaryllis in her tracks.

'Wherever did you hear such a thing, Betsy?'

'In church, last Sunday,' she explained matter-of-factly. 'I sit next to Dorcas. Ever since the young master came back from India, Dorcas hasn't paid *any* attention to the service.

'She keeps looking across at Mr

Adam in the Whitlocks' pew, but when *he* turns around and looks at her, Dorcas turns away and her face goes red.'

'I hadn't noticed anything like *that* going on!'

'Oh, yes,' nodded Betsy sagely. 'I have. For weeks. Anyhow, on Sunday, Great Aunt Macgregor must've noticed too, because when we were coming out from church she caught up with Dorcas. I didn't see the whole of their conversation, but they both looked really cross,' she continued solemnly. 'As they were parting at the gate, Great Aunt said, plain as anything, *'You're playing with fire, my girl — no good can come of setting your cap at the likes of Adam Whitlock!''*

★　★　★

Penelope continued reading aloud, but glanced across at her father. He'd finally drifted into sleep, his breathing steadier and quiet now.

16

Since earlier that year when Elias Whitlock was stricken by illness, there'd been many bad times when Penelope and her mother had sat up with him; last night had been yet another.

She moved across to one of the large windows. It was opened wide, the curtains drawn aside so soft morning light, birdsong and the heady fragrance of wallflowers, honeysuckle and roses drifted in with the warm late summer air. Penelope drank in a deep breath, gazing down upon the flower gardens of Haddonsell Grange.

They were Father's pride and joy!

Until his illness, whenever he wasn't working at the Akenside pottery or looking after estate affairs, Elias would be tending his flowers and caring for his bees. Regardless of weather or season, her father relished being outdoors, seeing the sky above him and breathing clear, fresh air.

He'd been born and bred in a pit village, and as a boy had laboured underground.

17

The bedroom door opened and Penelope turned from the window, whispering, 'Father's sleeping peacefully, but have you managed to have any rest?'

'I closed my eyes.' Dorothy Whitlock went to her daughter's side, gazing up into Penelope's drawn, pale face. 'My dear, I don't know how I would've managed these past months without you!

'And your father felt the same when you were taking care of everything at the pottery and here at Haddonsell,' she went on, sitting at his bedside with her knitting. 'Time and again, Elias'd say to me, '*There's naught to worry about with our Penny minding the shop for us, Dotty — All'll be well until Adam gets home and takes over,*' and that's exactly how it's turned out. You did a grand job of running things!'

'I only did what was needed,' smiled Penelope, dropping a kiss onto her mother's forehead. 'Since I was little, I've always enjoyed going to the pottery with Father and helping him around the estate. I was glad to do it.'

Stepping out onto the landing, she heard the door of Elias Whitlock's study downstairs opening and her brother and Gerrard emerging into the hallway. Low as their voices were, they carried distinctly.

'I certainly wasn't prepared to take *that* risk!' Adam was saying decisively.

'He left you with no choice, Adam. And this'll serve as warning to any — '

Noticing Penelope on the stairs, Gerrard's manner changed and he continued deferentially. 'Will there be anything else, sir?'

'No — no, thank you, Gerrard,' responded Adam, swiftly taking in the older man's darting glance toward the staircase. 'I'll join you presently.'

'Very good, sir.'

When Penelope came down into the hallway, Adam hurried to her.

'I believe Father was taken poorly again during the night. How is he?'

'Sleeping easy,' she reassured. 'Mother's with him.'

'I knew nothing about his having another bad turn until this morning! You should've roused me, Penelope! I might've been able to *do* something — '

'You *are* doing something,' she put in gently. 'You coming home to manage the family's affairs has lifted a great burden from Father's shoulders.

'I daresay this is selfish of me — because I know you've given up a good life in India — but I'm *very* happy you're home! We've missed you so much.' Penelope laughed softly. 'This old house has been abominably quiet without you!'

'Quiet and *peaceful*!' he responded wryly. 'I was wild and foolish and not the kindest of brothers, Penelope. I look back with shame and regret at the things I did and said.

'Furious as I was at being sent away, Father arranging that post in India was the making of me,' Adam confided soberly. 'It made a man of me. It made my fortune, too, for there are many opportunities in India for those with the wit to take them.'

'Running the pottery, the estate and so forth must be very different from your work in India,' she began tentatively. 'And I realise it isn't my place to interfere, but if I *can* do anything to help — '

'I won't hesitate to ask,' he interrupted. 'Now, I really must dash — Gerrard and I have a deal of work waiting!'

'Adam!' she cried uneasily. 'Adam, is — is all *well* with that man Gerrard?'

'Of course!' he returned sharply. 'Gerrard's my right-hand! He even saved my life once when we were caught up in a skirmish in India.

'He's somewhat rough around the edges and a bad loser at cards, but Gerrard's loyal and trustworthy,' continued Adam briskly. 'I depend on him, Penelope.'

'If you're *absolutely* sure — '

'I am,' grinned Adam, patting her shoulder. 'You're worn out. You should get some rest — and leave the canal, the pottery, the estate, the tenants and the rest of Father's cornucopia of interests and investments to *me*!'

★ ★ ★

Autumn was fast approaching and the dull day was chill with drifts of sea-fog creeping in from the distant tide. Ethel carried her tea, two billycans and two muslin-wrapped snaps of bread, cheese and onions out across the cobbled yard towards the stables.

'Joe!'

His head appeared through the open trapdoor from the loft. 'Up 'ere, missus!'

'I'll leave your snap on the ledge. Where's the master?'

'Digging taters!'

Nodding, Ethel went around the stables towards the fields behind the inn. Sandy was one-handedly pushing a barrowload of potatoes, with the dexterity and strength borne from years of hard work and perseverance. His maimed arm and scarred, twisted hand remained close against his right side. Sandy's weather-beaten features were set in concentration, a short clay pipe gripped between his teeth, as he kept the barrow balanced and brought it out from the field and around the path, his face breaking into a broad smile at the sight of his wife.

'I'm ready for this!' he said, unwrapping the bread and cheese when they were seated on the bench against the stables' sheltered wall.

Ethel sipped her tea. 'Your pipe's gone out.'

'It's not been lit!' he replied, biting into the fresh, crusty bread. 'I forgot to ask Am to fetch me some baccy when she was in St. Agnes. Oh, eh up, somebody's heading our way!'

'Why, it's young Mr Adam!' exclaimed Ethel, narrowing her eyes. 'He's not come from the Grange, either. I wonder what he wants?'

'We don't often see him here, that's for sure.'

'Well, it's high time we did!' returned

Ethel briskly, hastily rising and smoothing her shawl and skirts. 'The young master's been back a fair few months. Long enough for him to be a regular visitor to The Bell, as was his dear father before he took ill.

'Having gentry like the Whitlocks here does wonders for the inn's reputation, Sandy,' she persisted. 'Word gets around and brings in quality folk — the sort of folk we *want* at The Bell — instead of some of the raggle-taggle locals who practically take root here day in, day out!'

'I daresay,' commented Sandy with sigh. 'I'd best go and see to him.'

'Can't you smarten yourself up a bit?' She considered him critically. 'Mr Adam is an important gentleman, and you look a right sight!'

'I've been digging taters, not at church!' protested Sandy, nonetheless dusting down his coat and straightening his collar as he hurried around to the front of the inn.

'Encourage him to stay a while!'

24

called Ethel, scurrying toward the big kitchen. 'Ask him if he'd like some dinner — *luncheon*, that is . . . '

Sandy was waiting before the inn to greet Adam Whitlock when he rode up.

'Good day, Mr Adam! Welcome to The Bell. What can we do for you?'

'I'm taking the Lancaster coach, Macgregor,' said Adam Whitlock, dismounting. 'I've been out since early morning and am chilled to the marrow, famished and generally in need of sustenance!'

'We've a good blaze and a hearty bill of fare ready and waiting,' the innkeeper replied cheerfully.

'My word, that fire is indeed a welcome sight!' exclaimed Adam, removing his wide-brimmed hat and pushing his riding gloves into the side pocket of his greatcoat as he accompanied Sandy into The Bell.

'Sit yourself down, sir. I'll take your hat and coat,' Sandy beckoned Amaryllis to hurry forward to receive them. 'Can I fetch you tea or coffee?'

25

'Something rather stronger,' grinned Adam. 'A hot toddy — and a dish of whatever those fellows over there are eating. It smells delicious!'

★　★　★

Several short blasts of the coachman's horn heralded the vehicle's approach and Amaryllis scurried to Adam Whitlock's table, bobbing a respectful curtsy.

'The coach is on its way, sir. I'll fetch your coat.'

Going through the arch into the long passageway, she almost collided with Dorcas who was flying along with a basket of freshly-pressed linen clutched in her arms.

'Why didn't you tell me Adam Whitlock was here?' she demanded accusingly, her face flushed with anger. 'Why didn't you *tell* me, Am?'

'Why would I tell you?' shrugged Amaryllis, carefully lifting the hat and great coat from the rack.

'Is that *his* coat?'

Dropping the linen basket, Dorcas reached out to take hold of the garment but her keen eyes lit upon a pair of gloves, protruding from the side pocket. In a flash, she'd withdrawn them, clasping them tightly with both hands.

'Dorcas!' gasped Amaryllis in horror. 'What on earth are you doing?'

'Mind your own business and take Mr Adam his coat,' Dorcas's eyes narrowed warningly. 'Then stay out of my way!'

Amaryllis hovered uncertainly, the coat heavy in her arms. She had no notion of what Dorcas intended to do. 'Give me the gloves, Dorcas — '

'Am! What's keeping you, girl?' Sandy called down the passageway. 'Mr Adam's waiting!'

'Coming, Pa!' replied Amaryllis distractedly, darting a backward glance to her sister as she sped through to the inn.

'Sorry to keep you, Mr Adam,' she murmured, her eyes lowered. 'Safe journey, sir.'

When the coach was ready to resume its journey and Adam about to alight, Dorcas suddenly emerged from the inn, her red-gold ringlets tumbling about her shoulders.

'Mr Adam!' she called, hurrying to his side and dipping a pretty curtsy. 'Beg pardon, sir — I believe your gloves have fallen from your coat . . .'

From one of the inn's small-paned windows, Amaryllis watched open-mouthed, scarcely able to believe her eyes. She saw Adam Whitlock smile, reaching out his hand for the gloves — and it seemed to Amaryllis that Dorcas's hand lingered upon those gloves far longer than necessary.

Both parties were smiling now, and it was clear pleasantries were being exchanged.

'What are you looking at?' queried Betsy, ducking under Amaryllis's arm so she too could peer from the little window.

Before Amaryllis could reply, her elder sister swept back into the inn, looking thoroughly pleased with herself. Head held high, her cheeks rosy and green eyes sparkling, Dorcas Macgregor sauntered past them without a word.

★ ★ ★

From the small square window of the wooden hut he called his office, Kit Chesterton noticed the lady seated some distance away on a ridge above the wide, swift-flowing River Aken.

Her grey mare grazed patiently while she sketched the work underway on the spur of waterway which was to connect the manufacturing town of Akenside with the Leeds Liverpool Canal.

It wasn't until she'd moved down from the ridge, however, and was drawing the workings from a different angle, that Kit saw the lady's features clearly. He recognised her at once. Miss Whitlock had accompanied her father to a number of meetings during the Cut's proposal and planning, and they'd met again when she and her parents had attended the ceremonial sod-turning.

Kit had heard Elias Whitlock was seriously ill, and was deeply sorry. He'd found the elderly man to be honest, plain-spoken and fired with an almost boyish enthusiasm that reminded Kit of his own father's attitude — or at least, the attitude of Thomas Chesterton, whom he'd *believed* to be his father . . .

When Kit had occasion to quit his office, Penelope glanced up, raising her hand in greeting.

'My apologies, Miss Whitlock,' he began, approaching her. 'I didn't wish to disturb you.'

'You haven't, Mr Chesterton! I've completed what I came to do,' she replied amiably, closing her sketch-book. 'My father and I were speaking about the Akenside Cut yesterday, and I had the notion of riding over and making a few drawings so he might gain an inkling of how the Cut's taking shape.'

'What a splendid idea,' responded

Kit, adding impulsively, 'would you care to see where the wharf is being built?'

'Indeed I would!' she replied, packing her drawing materials into a canvas bag and fastening it securely behind Sorrel's saddle.

'This is the first time I've been here since we came for the sod-turning,' Penelope was saying while they walked across the workings. 'I'm afraid Father's feeling very dispirited and out of touch with — well, with *all* of his interests and occupations.

'He'll be pleased at how efficiently the Cut is progressing.' She glanced up at Kit, smiling. 'And even *more* impatient to recover so he might come and see everything for himself!'

'Mr Whitlock worked tirelessly and never once wavered in his determination to see the Akenside Cut constructed,' recalled Kit. 'Over the months, he and I had many interesting conversations — sometimes even upon subjects *other* than canals!'

Laughing, Penelope hesitated a fraction before continuing. 'Mr Chesterton, I don't suppose you'd care to call upon Father? He'd thoroughly enjoy talking to you again and — ' She broke off, colour flooding her pale face. 'Forgive me! I spoke without thought! You have a great many demands upon — '

'Miss Whitlock,' interrupted Kit quietly, his serious eyes meeting hers. 'I'd very much like the opportunity to renew my acquaintance with your father.'

★   ★   ★

The November morning that Kit called upon Elias Whitlock at Haddonsell Grange was cold and dismal, with a cutting north-westerly wind.

Elias was delighted with the books Kit brought as get-well gifts, and soon absorbed in the engineer's surveys and diagrams of the Cut's construction, which had advanced considerably since Elias had seen the initial specifications.

Around midday, a beaming Mrs Dorothy Whitlock brought in a luncheon tray, announcing that as a rare treat, Elias was being allowed small helpings of his favourite foods!

Elias's haggard features positively lit up at the sight of the dishes.

'This is luxury indeed, Chesterton,' he said, when the two men were enjoying their meal. 'I'm usually on invalid's rations — Dr Baldwin's orders — gruel and other slop! I haven't eaten such miserable fare since I was a boy, when victuals of any description were far and few between . . . '

He fell to reminiscing about his boyhood in the pit village and how, like many a penniless lad, he'd gone down to Liverpool in search of work and the means of making his way in the world. In return, Kit found himself speaking of his own early years, and of his family in Jamaica.

'Jamaica?' exclaimed Elias, grinning broadly. 'You're from Jamaica, Kit?

'Why, when I was young and in the

employ of a Liverpool potter, I sailed to Jamaica! Mr Standish had dealings with a merchant there who catered for rich folks' tastes, and he sent me over with crates of luxury goods for the plantation mansions and suchlike.

'Jamaica,' he sighed, those carefree, adventurous days bright and clear in his memory. 'Always planned to go back, y'know . . . Never did, though.'

* * *

Mindful of the elderly man's frail health, Kit was concerned not to overtire Mr Whitlock and hadn't intended a lengthy visit. However, the companionable hours had slipped away unnoticed until Kit finally bade Elias farewell and took his leave late in the wintry afternoon.

He rode slowly down the beech drive from the Grange and out between the gates, but instead of heading inland to his lodgings in Akenside, Kit impulsively veered westward.

Cantering away to the windswept coastline, he gave the swift piebald mare her head until they approached an inn perched on the cliff-top. Slowing to a walk, they passed The Bell and followed the steep, curving sweep of Macgregor's Cove. Up here, the keen, salt-sharp sea wind gusted ice cold against Kit's face, the thump and surge of the incoming high tide pounding in his ears as he rode on beyond the cove.

He paused on high ground above a small boatyard, which looked as though it had seen far better days. A lone man was sawing timber. With the task completed, he straightened up, easing the stiffness from his back before hefting the timber and carrying it toward a shed. Glancing up, he noticed Kit and raised an arm; the two strangers exchanged a pleasant greeting before the grey-haired man let himself into the boatyard's tiny cottage. A moment later, a dim light flickered into life beyond the thick glass of a small, crooked window.

Sensible to the darkening November sky, Kit turned and started back the way he'd come.

Inexplicably, his thoughts were straying to Jamaica, to the bundle of faded love letters . . . to Marietta's humble keepsake. Drawing a measured breath, he stared out across miles of open sea to the brigs, schooners, clippers, barques and all manner of smaller vessels sailing with the tide and following wind for Liverpool Bay; navigating the hazardous course toward the Mersey river and thence into port.

Almost directly below Kit and hugging the ragged coastline was a two-masted yawl. From his vantage point on the cliff-top, the craft resembled a child's toy held together with string and sealing wax, tossed and deluged by wind and water as it rounded the crag and disappeared from view. Riding at a canter now, for daylight was fast fading, he followed the deep curve of the cove and presently spied the glowing lamps of The Bell.

Kit could make out three figures approaching the inn from the opposite direction. A woman carrying a basket over her arm was holding the hand of a little girl; they were hurrying along from the quayside, heads bowed into the blustery wind, their cloaks and skirts billowing. Beside them scampered a small white dog, first running a little way ahead, then turning about and returning to the little girl, who each time stooped to pat and praise it.

Suddenly the child spun around and cried out, tugging at the woman's arm and pointing away into the dark, churning tide. Kit could not see whatever she saw, but the woman did.

Dropping the basket and hitching her skirts, she ran for all she was worth toward the inn, the little girl and dog at her heels.

Even as Kit was galloping up to the cove's headland, he heard the splitting and tearing of timber; the cries and shouts of men and women in terror for their lives.

A mournful wailing rang out through the gathering dusk and Kit spun around from the cliff's edge.

Amaryllis Macgregor was tolling the inn's great brass bell, summoning help for those in peril on the sea.

2

'Ammie, come and see!' called Betsy. She and Flossie had clambered up onto the oak blanket chest beside the oblong window on the inn's top landing.

'Uncle Iain's putting out his boat — and that new man with the spotted horse is going with him!'

'What new man?' queried Amaryllis distractedly, turning from the linen cupboard and darting to her sister's side, a bundle of clean towels in her arms.

'The man who was on the cliff riding this way when you rang the bell,' explained Betsy, pointing out into the gathering darkness. 'There they are! Uncle Iain's rowing and the new man has a lantern, see?'

Amaryllis could barely make out Iain Macgregor's row-boat striving against the ferocity of a high, incoming tide

— nor the two shadowy figures aboard.

'Will you take these towels downstairs, while I get lots of blankets?' she asked, shepherding Betsy towards the crooked stairs. 'Everybody will be coming back to the inn, and they'll be cold and wet so we must be ready for them!'

Alone on the landing, Amaryllis gazed from the oblong window. She could no longer see Uncle Iain's boat, only the beam of his companion's lantern held aloft, swinging back and forth across the black water; searching for survivors. Another two boats were setting out now, and in a moment they too would be swallowed up into the moonless night with only their lanterns pinpricking the darkness.

Laden with heavy blankets, Amaryllis reached the foot of the steep staircase as her mother was scurrying towards the passageway through to the inn-house.

'Good girl, you've got the blankets! Put them to warm with the towels.

Your Pa and Joe have taken the waggon down onto the shore to bring back the rescued folk. I'm nipping next-door to fetch Betsy's drawing book and pencils,' Ethel related rapidly, scarce slowing her pace. 'The lass's all right, but she had a fright seeing that boat going down. Once I get her warm and settled in the chimney corner with Flossie and a hot drink and her drawing, she'll be grand.

'Dorcas is heating honey and milk for her . . . '

Amaryllis could hear Dorcas talking to Widow Watkins as she hurried past the inn's big kitchen. Going through the arch, she was met by a cold blast of damp salt air. The Bell's low front door was flung wide open. Betsy and Flossie were out on the doorstone, peering into the night.

'It's freezing out here! Come on in, pet,' Amaryllis slipped her arm about Betsy's shoulders. 'Pa won't be back for a while yet.'

'We're not waiting for Pa,' she replied, looking up at her sister solemnly. 'We're watching the spotted horse — she's running round the yard, Ammie!'

★ ★ ★

Amaryllis had rubbed down the piebald mare, settled her into a stall and fed her when she heard the waggon's wheels rumbling over the yard's cobbles and dashed outside, the feed pail still in her hands.

'Pa!'

'All's well!' he called, driving on to the inn.

She glimpsed six people from the stricken yawl huddled into the waggon bed. Following on foot were her uncle and the man whom Betsy said owned the stray horse, together with several other local men who'd put out rescue boats.

'Sir!' she fell into step beside Uncle Iain and the stranger. 'Is the piebald yours? She found her way into our yard. I've tended her, and she's in the stable yonder.'

'Thank you kindly, miss — I'm obliged!' exclaimed Kit, shaking his head ruefully. 'When I heard that bell tolling, I'm afraid I abandoned poor Patch on the cliff-top — '

'And ran down to help me launch the boat,' chipped in Iain heartily. 'Glad I am of it, too!'

'Pa said all was well?' queried Amaryllis quickly, when the waggon drew to a halt and Iain and the other men hurried forward to help the survivors indoors.

'The yawl's lad took a bit of a battering, the rest o'em are walking wounded,' Iain responded, as he and Kit Chesterton half-carried the craft's bosun into The Bell.

'No lives were lost to the sea *this* night!'

★ ★ ★

43

Ethel moved noiselessly about the snug, where the badly injured young sailor had been carried. Gathering up the bowls of water, cloths, bindings and medicaments she'd used to bathe and salve his cuts and bruises, she turned at a soft tapping upon the door.

'Thought you might be ready for this, Ma,' whispered Amaryllis, tiptoeing inside with a cup of freshly-brewed tea. 'How is he?'

'In a bad way, Am. Your pa reckons the current must've thrown him against the yawl's broken timbers. I've given poppy syrup for the pain and to make him sleep, but there's naught more I can do,' replied Ethel bleakly, tucking the warm blankets about him more closely. 'This lad needs proper doctoring.'

'Even if he's out on a call, Dr Baldwin will surely have heard the bell tolling,' reassured Amaryllis. 'He's likely on his way.'

'I expect you're right,' Ethel sighed heavily, adding, 'How are the others?'

'Dorcas put the womenfolk upstairs in one of the rooms and found them dry clothing. They're resting. The old man had a nasty gash so Widow Watkins tended him while I saw to the rest,' related Amaryllis quietly. 'The rescuers are all safe. Everybody's getting dry around the fire now, and Widow Watkins is dishing up soup and bannocks.'

'Don't let Freda overdo it, Am. She isn't as young as she was,' remarked Ethel. Widow Watkins had helped her at The Bell for more years than either of them cared count. The elderly woman lived in, with a room at the top of the back stairs directly above the inn's big kitchen.

'Noah will be bringing in the packet shortly,' went on Ethel, moving from the injured boy's side. 'We'd best get a move on. There'll be passengers needing attention.'

'Dorcas and I can do that, Ma. You stay here, in case he needs you.'

'Truth to tell, I *am* loath to leave

45

him,' murmured Ethel, her watchful gaze upon the sailor's still face. 'He's so young, Am! Scarce more'n a bairn. Some poor mother's son — I hope to heaven Dr Baldwin gets here soon!'

*   *   *

Amaryllis was hurrying back and forth from the big kitchen when Noah Pendleton brought in the packet from the Isle of Man. As always, he tooted the sturdy vessel's horn before mooring at the quayside and shepherding his passengers up into the welcoming light and warmth of The Bell.

Glancing around at hearing Noah calling her name, Amaryllis saw him striding towards her as she weaved between tables, balancing a huge tray of steaming hot-pots and a sizeable jug of brandy.

'Let me take that lot — it looks heavy!'

'I can manage,' she responded with a quick smile, swiftly serving a batch of meals before turning to a settle nearest the door with the brandy jug, another hot-pot and an enormous sweet pie. 'He's gone!'

'Who's gone?'

'The fisherman who ordered all this!' returned Amaryllis, searching the crowded inn. 'He was first in from the packet. Tall and thin, with a thick beard.

'There's no sign of him!' she finished, tutting in vexation. 'Noah, would you please take these?'

Handing him the brandy jug and plates of uneaten food, Amaryllis started for the big kitchen, deftly heaping the tray with empty mugs, glasses, crocks and cutlery as she went.

'Was it a rough crossing today?' she asked over her shoulder.

'We've had smoother,' said Noah, looking across to the chimney corner, where Betsy was engrossed in playing a game.

'Your pa told me you and Betsy saw the yawl going down,' he went on, following Amaryllis into the big kitchen. 'That's a terrible sight to see, Am. Are you both all right?'

'We've had lots to do tonight, and keeping busy helps,' she answered simply, looking up into his anxious eyes. 'It was Betsy who spotted the yawl was in trouble, Noah. I hadn't noticed a thing. It was *Betsy* who raised the alarm!'

'The folk aboard that yawl owe the little lass their lives,' he remarked. Gravely, he added, 'And you're sure she's all right?'

Amaryllis nodded, smiling warmly at him. 'Betsy's been drawing spotted horses in her book, and now she's playing spillikins with Uncle Iain!'

'Who's that stranger with them?'

'Mr Chesterton from Akenside. He went out in the boat with Uncle Iain — '

'Another seven hot-pots, four soups and a pot of tea for ten,' announced Dorcas briskly, sweeping into the big kitchen with a heap of dirty dishes for washing. 'And *more* pasties — I swear, some of these people can't have eaten for months!'

'You take the pasties,' responded Amaryllis, heading for the simmering soup cauldron. 'I'll bring out the rest!'

When Dorcas had gone and he and Amaryllis were alone again, Noah drew breath to speak but hesitated, saying nothing. Frowning, he watched Amaryllis absorbed in her work: ladling soup into basins; filling a great teapot, placing cups, sugar dishes and milk jugs onto trays; stooping to withdraw a board laden with hot-pots from the warming oven.

'I'll carry it!' Finding his voice, Noah stepped forward.

'Thanks,' she responded, taking the soups and tea tray. 'That's a big help!'

With the food and drink duly served, they were making their way to the big kitchen when Noah cleared his throat.

'Am, yesterday I was in Miss Macgregor's bookshop and she showed me a handbill about the dramatic

49

society's new play. Your great aunt said it's a very good play,' he went on in a rush. 'It opens tomorrow evening and I was wondering if — that is, if you'd like — '

Amaryllis wasn't listening.

She'd turned on her heel, looking across the crowded inn to its low front door. Her father and a portly figure were crossing the threshold.

'Dr Baldwin's here — thank goodness!' murmured Amaryllis, watching the two men hurrying round to the snug and offering a silent prayer for the young sailor's wellbeing.

'Noah,' she began thoughtfully, when they entered the quietness of the big kitchen. 'Have you heard from Simon lately?

'When he first took up that important post at the shipping office and moved to Liverpool, Simon wrote regularly. I write to him every week and, of course, I do realise he's very busy with his work there,' Amaryllis reasoned, stacking dirty plates and pots into the tub for washing. 'But I haven't had a letter for months and — and I'm worried about him.

'Have *you* news of him, Noah? You and Simon were inseparable.'

'As lads, maybe. But it's long since we played hide-and-go-seek in the old smugglers' tunnels!' Noah shook his head wryly. 'Me and Simon Baldwin went our separate ways years ago, Am. He's no reason to get in touch with me.'

'I see,' she sighed, returning to the chores. As an afterthought, she added, 'Oh, what were you saying earlier about Great Aunt's bookshop?'

'Nothing important,' responded Noah, his gaze lingering upon her a little longer than the words he uttered. Finally, he turned away. 'Reckon I'd best be heading home. Goodnight, Amaryllis.'

★   ★   ★

'It's been a queer old day and no mistake,' ruminated Iain Macgregor,

51

staring out into the dark night.

'Can't argue with that,' Kit reflected. He was seated across the square table in The Bell's window alcove.

That afternoon, when he'd been riding from Haddonsell Grange and had impulsively headed out along the coast toward the boatyard, Kit had had Marietta's letters very much in his thoughts — together with the knowledge that Alexander Macgregor had lived at his family's boatyard in the cove.

Upon sight of a grey-haired man working there and entering the boatyard cottage, Kit had assumed *he* might be Alexander Macgregor. Now, he knew differently.

'I'd best stir my stumps and make tracks,' commented Iain, showing no sign of stirring anything at all. 'Sandy said you're staying here tonight?'

'Yes,' nodded Kit. He and Sandy Macgregor *had* met — albeit briefly — after the rush and commotion following the rescue had subsided. It

52

had, to borrow Iain's words, been a queer old encounter. Arranging mundane accommodation, while looking straight into the face of a man who was perhaps his father — and realising this man had not the slightest suspicion they might be flesh and blood — had shaken Kit far more deeply than he could ever have anticipated.

'Yes,' he repeated, and not for the first time that evening, his gaze strayed toward Sandy Macgregor, who was genially waiting upon locals, regulars, travellers and strangers alike as The Bell gradually settled back into the bustling, homely routine of a small country inn.

'I'm putting up here for a few days,' continued Kit with his quick smile. 'It's a most agreeable and hospitable establishment.'

'You should have seen The Bell when me and Sandy were lads!' exclaimed Iain unexpectedly. 'We were born and bred like generations of Macgregors at the boatyard yonder, and this inn'd had a gruesome reputation for a hundred years and more.'

'Why so?'

'The Bell was a den of smugglers, wreckers and cut-throats,' he answered grimly. 'Terrible, it was. No honest folk dared set foot anywhere near. They were too frightened.

'It wasn't until Elias Whitlock moved into Haddonsell Grange and become magistrate that things started changing. He swore he'd bring the thieves and murderers to justice and stamp out smuggling and wrecking along this stretch of coast once and for all.

'Elias'd have nowt to do with taking back-handers to turn a blind eye like many another before him had done, so *that* made him powerful enemies!' Iain recalled soberly. 'It near cost Elias Whitlock his life more'n once, but he finally rid this cove of villainy.'

'Was that when your brother took over The Bell?'

Iain shook his head, drawing on his pipe. 'The place stood empty for years.

54

Because of the evil goings-on, nobody would touch it with a bargepole. Then after Sandy got home from the Navy, he surprised us by turning innkeeper!'

'The Navy, you say . . . ?'

'Aye, that's right. He's done a grand job,' went on Iain, and there was no mistaking the pride in his voice. 'The Bell's a fine inn, and Sandy's made a good life and home for his family here, too. After everything he went through, there's nobody deserves it more.'

Iain lapsed into silence, and Kit was left pondering. So Sandy had served in the King's Navy . . . But had he ever sailed to Jamaica?

'Your room's ready, sir.'

Sandy Macgregor's voice broke into Kit's deliberations.

He started, suddenly meeting Sandy's eyes. 'Ah! Thank you!'

'You mentioned you'll be working while you're here,' went on Sandy. 'We've put you in the big corner room. It has a little parlour adjoining with a writing table and suchlike.'

'That's thoughtful,' replied Kit, clearing his throat. 'I'm obliged.'

'You're welcome, sir. If you need anything, just let us know,' Sandy turned to Iain, grinning. 'We can put you up an' all — save ye the long walk home!'

'Nay, I like my own bed,' Iain rose stiffly, offering his hand to Kit. 'I'll say goodnight, Mr Chesterton. Thanks for coming out in the boat today — it's a job as needs more'n one pair of hands!'

Talking as they went, the brothers crossed the inn, disappearing from Kit's sight.

He expelled a measured breath. Had he found — and met — his father? If so, what on earth was he to *do* about Sandy Macgregor?

Mechanically, Kit poured another cup from the coffee pot. The strong black liquid was nearly cold now, but he didn't notice.

His brooding gaze wandered to Amaryllis and Dorcas, busily refilling cups and tankards and clearing dishes and plates, and to Betsy, the little deaf girl, curled up with her dog in the chimney corner.

Three strangers who, quite possibly, were his sisters.

★ ★ ★

Ethel was content with her lot in life.

She enjoyed helping Sandy run The Bell, and while she took great pride in preparing the inn's fare in its big bustling kitchen, the shiny-as-a-new-pin little kitchen in the inn-house was *her* kitchen — the heart of her family's home — and Ethel was never happier than when she was cooking and baking there.

She was in especially cheery spirit today because not only was the young lad from the yawl recovered enough to have gone home up-coast, but Dorcas had an admirer — and he was a real feather in her eldest daughter's cap!

Ethel's eyes were sharp, and she'd long since noticed glances and smiles being exchanged between Dorcas and Adam Whitlock during his visits to The Bell — which were becoming more and more frequent — and at church, too. After services yesterday, Dorcas had left her book — accidentally on purpose, Ethel surmised! — behind in the pew and none other than the young master himself had hurried after her to return it.

Ethel was almost certain she'd glimpsed a note tucked amongst the book's leaves. A message arranging a rendezvous, perhaps?

Dorcas hadn't breathed a word, of course, but the girl's obvious excitement and heightened colour spoke volumes. Ethel didn't ask any questions today when Dorcas had dressed in her best and set off for St. Agnes.

Ethel's fervent hopes went with her.

There'd been little romance or prospects in her own young days, and nobody could deny the handsome, chivalrous heir to the Whitlock fortune would be a catch for the finest young lady in the county, much less the daughter of a humble innkeeper.

Yes, thought Ethel, fetching flour, sugar, fruit and spices from the pantry as Betsy ran into the little kitchen to help bake an apple dumpling cake; if this romance with Adam Whitlock blossomed into marriage, Dorcas would be assured a comfortable and secure future.

A mother couldn't wish better for her daughter.

★   ★   ★

There wasn't a breath of wind as Kit cantered towards Haddonsell Grange, and the bare trees overarching the winding lane were sparkling with hard, white frost.

Beyond the curve, he saw Miss Whitlock walking some distance ahead. Despite the earliness of the hour, Kit wasn't at all surprised to see her because during one of their conversations, Elias Whitlock had mentioned his daughter was a keen walker who relished being out and about first thing in the morning while the world was still quiet. Catching up with her, Kit greeted Penelope amiably.

'Good morning, Miss Whitlock! I too am on my way to the Grange. May I walk with you?'

'Please do!' She upturned her face, smiling at him as he dismounted, and Kit was taken aback at the becoming roses in her cheeks and how particularly blue Penelope's eyes appeared in this bright winter sunlight. 'Father said you'd be calling — he has the chess board ready and waiting!'

Kit grimaced good-humouredly. 'We paused our game at a critical stage, and I suspect your father has the beating of me!'

'He enjoys your visits very much, Mr Chesterton. Although Father's health is extremely frail, his mind and spirit are strong. He looks forward to your stimulating discussions — and your chess games!' She smiled at Kit again.

'You're still staying at The Bell?'

'I am. Actually, I'm quitting my lodgings in Akenside and removing to The Bell,' answered Kit, and fancying he saw surprise flitting across Penelope's expressive face, continued quickly. 'It isn't the most practical of decisions, because it entails travelling back and forth from the Cut each day — '

'Oh, but practicality isn't everything! Besides, the distance is not so great,' interjected Penelope earnestly. 'If, instead of travelling by road, you rode across country.'

'I didn't know there was such a route!'

'It's not well-trod and in places barely wide enough for a horse and rider, but there *is* a path through the hills,' she explained enthusiastically. 'If you wish, I'll gladly show you the way.'

'That would be splendid!' He paused, before adding a shade tentatively, 'Might we go tomorrow? If you're free, that is?'

'Tomorrow will be perfect,' declared Penelope, beaming sidelong at him. 'And for what it's worth, Mr Chesterton, I believe your moving into The Bell is an *excellent* decision!'

★ ★ ★

' . . . so it's the first time Simon won't be with us gathering evergreens and bringing home the yule log,' grumbled Amaryllis, while she and her mother were dusting and polishing Kit Chesterton's spacious corner rooms at The Bell. 'This year, it'll be just Noah and me!'

'Don't forget Flossie and I!' chipped in Betsy indignantly, carefully carrying a stone ink bottle to top up the wells on the sturdy writing table. '*We're* coming this afternoon!'

'You'll be in charge of the picnic basket,' responded Amaryllis, smiling down at the little girl and tugging her pigtails. 'Collecting evergreens for Advent wouldn't be the same without our winter picnic at St. Agnes's waterfall!'

'Too true,' agreed Ethel, helping Betsy steady the heavy stone bottle while she poured the ink. 'And we need *plenty* of greenery to deck the church — it looked a bit sparse last year, I thought — as well as enough for the inn and the inn-house, so you'll all be kept very busy today!'

★　★　★

Noah Pendleton arrived promptly, driving the heavy cart borrowed from his family's grain mill. The traditional winter picnic basket was duly loaded, and everybody piled into the cart. Noah jiggled the reins, broke into an old seasonal song and off they set.

> *I'll sing you one, O*
> *Green grow the rushes, O*
> *What is your one, O?*
> *One is one and —*

Amaryllis and Betsy lost no time

joining in with Noah's rich baritone and their jubilant singing filled the chill December air as the cart rumbled along the cliff-path.

They'd barely started into the verse about seven stars in the sky when rapidly approaching hoofbeats caused Noah to pause and glance behind them. A familiar voice hailed him, and Simon Baldwin galloped up alongside the cart, slightly breathless from the hard ride and grinning from ear to ear.

'Simon!' cried Amaryllis joyfully, her excited eyes huge and shining. 'You're back!'

'Fresh from the Liverpool coach,' he answered blithely, sliding from the saddle and tying the sweating horse's reins onto the mill cart. 'I asked where you were, and when Mrs Macgregor told me you'd gone for the Advent evergreens, I borrowed this nag and here I am!'

Simon didn't appear to notice the thunderous glare Noah Pendleton threw his way as he leapt aboard the cart, squeezing onto the makeshift seat beside Amaryllis and launching into an amusing anecdote about his life and work in Liverpool.

St. Agnes's ancient woodland lay inland some distance beyond the ruins. It was reached by crossing a narrow stone bridge, and skirting around the remains of the cloister and away past the medieval priory's crumbling infirmary.

' . . . we'll leave the cart in the usual spot,' Noah remarked tersely. Other than passing the time of day with his boyhood pal, he hadn't spoken a word since Simon Baldwin had invited himself along on the outing. 'I've brought ropes and sacking to haul the yule — '

'What business are *they* about?' interrupted Simon, pointing toward the ruins. 'It's rare seeing *anybody* up here, much less a pair of the blighters!'

'The stockier fellow is Gerrard from the Grange,' answered Noah, glancing around to Amaryllis. 'I don't recognise the one with the beard though, do you?'

Amaryllis shook her head, looking hard at the tall, thin man clad in fisherman's garb. 'But I'm certain I've seen him before . . .

'At The Bell — the night the yawl went down!' she exclaimed suddenly. 'That's *definitely* him! He came in on the Isle of Man packet, ordered a *huge* meal and a whole jug of brandy — then vanished!

'Whyever would a Manx fisherman be at the ruins with the Whitlocks' new bailiff?' she mused. 'And as Simon said — what can they be *doing* up here?'

Noah shrugged, his attention fixed upon Gerrard and the fisherman. They'd emerged from the cloister and although still some yards away, were effectively blocking the cart's progress.

Noah had already slowed; now he drew to a halt.

'Good day, Miss Macgregor. Gentlemen,' greeted Gerrard cordially, sauntering toward them. 'I must request you turn about and return the way you've come

— you're trespassing upon private property, y'know!'

'*Trespassing?*' echoed Simon incredulously, looking down at him. 'Don't be absurd, man!'

'As I daresay you're well aware,' went on Gerrard, his lilting brogue indulgent. 'This *is* Whitlock land, sir.'

'Of course it is!' Simon retorted angrily. 'Look, I haven't the slightest idea who you are, but we — my friends and I — have since childhood visited these ruins and the priory's woodland *with* Mr Whitlock's full knowledge and consent — '

'That's as may be, sir,' — although his tone remained civil, the bailiff took several strides nearer the cart before standing fast — 'but you *are* trespassing, and you're *not* going a foot further!'

'I demand an — '

'Leave it, Simon!' warned Noah in a low voice, nodding acquiescence to the bailiff. 'There's naught more to be done here.'

'Noah's right,' Amaryllis murmured suddenly, her arm tightening protectively about Betsy's shoulders.

From the tail of her eye, she'd been observing not Gerrard, but his silent ally. The fisherman, who was standing a few yards aside, appearing bored by the discourse as he leaned a shoulder to a crumbling pillar and chewed tobacco.

Shifting his weight, he spat the dark tobacco juice into the coarse marram grass, and in that slightest movement Amaryllis caught the dull gleam of a pistol tucked into his belt beneath the thick fustian coat.

'Let's go home,' she urged unsteadily, her heart pounding as she drew Betsy even closer against her.

'Let's go home, Noah!'

★　★　★

Penelope Whitlock was already dressed in a sensible hat and thick coat and about to set out for St. Agnes when her maid brought in a letter, just arrived with the morning's post.

Recognising the handwriting as that of her dearest friend, Penelope immediately broke the seal and unfolded a single sheet of notepaper.

'Not bad news, I hope,' murmured Margaret, watching her mistress's forehead creasing into an anxious frown. 'The letter *is* from Miss Lydia, isn't it?'

'Yes . . . Yes, Mag. It is,' replied Penelope, glancing up from the half-dozen sentences obviously penned with greatest haste. The Unsworth and Whitlock families had been close friends for years. She and Lydia had grown up together, and to this day remained as intimate as sisters. Lydia Unsworth was a gay, spirited soul but she certainly was *not* given to flights of fancy or melodrama, and yet . . .

Penelope's worried gaze returned to the letter.

My dear friend,
There's been the most shocking row.
Everything here has changed.

I must get away from Skilbeck, Penny!
May I come to Haddonsell for a while?
I will confide all when I see you.
Affectionately yours, Lydia

'Lydia is coming to stay, Mag. Will you please prepare her usual room?' began Penelope, hurrying to her writing slope and taking up her pen. 'I shall reply at once. Something is gravely amiss over at Skilbeck!'

★   ★   ★

Within the hour, Penelope was in St. Agnes. Her response to Lydia's heartfelt plea was aboard the fast mail coach and on its way to the Unsworth family estate of Skilbeck.

She fulfilled several errands before crossing the town square to Mathilda Macgregor's stationer and bookshop. She pushed open the narrow door and set the small bell jangling.

'Good afternoon, Miss Macgregor,' smiled Penelope. 'I wondered if the novel you recommended for Father has arrived?'

'Good afternoon. Yes, it came this morning.' Mathilda Macgregor was not a woman to mince words, and continued briskly. 'Miss Whitlock, the church will look extremely bare without its St. Agnes evergreens!

'Amaryllis and young Betsy went with Noah Pendleton and Dr Baldwin's son to gather Advent greenery from the priory's woodland — as they do every year — only to be accused of trespass and ordered from the ruins by Haddonsell's bailiff and a fisherman who, although taking no actual part in the altercation, was *armed!*

'If you'll forgive my bluntness,' she met the younger woman's horrified gaze stonily, 'it's nothing short of disgraceful for Macgregors and their companions to be treated as common criminals!'

'I know nothing of this, Miss Macgregor. Nor does my father,' gasped Penelope. 'It's appalling! My father wouldn't — '

'Mr *Elias* Whitlock certainly wouldn't, but . . . ' Mathilda left the sentence unfinished.

'My brother would neither order nor countenance such conduct, Miss Macgregor,' put in Penelope severely. 'I assure you of that!'

Mathilda inclined her head slightly, remarking, 'Then that new man of his appears to be taking the law into his own hands, does he not?'

*   *   *

Hurrying homewards through the chill rain, Penelope dwelled upon her conversation with Mathilda Macgregor.

She'd never trusted Gerrard!

Almost since he'd first arrived at Haddonsell Grange, a vague uneasiness had frayed at the edges of Penelope's consciousness.

While Gerrard might well have been Adam's agent in India, there was nothing of the master and subordinate

72

about their association. Neither were the two men friends, for Penelope had witnessed no affection nor camaraderie between them. But there was certainly *something* . . . Something that didn't seem quite right.

Why had Adam brought Gerrard from India and installed him as bailiff at Haddonsell?

He'd once told her that Gerrard had saved his life in India.

Did her brother's sense of being beholden — *indebted* — explain his offering the older man not only a situation of authority, but also a home at the Grange?

Or was the true reason far more sinister?

A chilling suspicion was taking shape in Penelope's thoughts. Before he'd left England as a youth, her brother had been wild and reckless. But Adam was *still* very young — only five-and-twenty. Had he foolishly committed further misdeeds or indiscretions in India, of which Gerrard had knowledge?

73

Did this man possess intelligence that could bring down scandal, dishonour and shame upon Adam and the Whitlock family?

Penelope's heart was hammering as she entered the gates of Haddonsell and hurried toward the house.

Was Gerrard *blackmailing* her headstrong and vulnerable younger brother?

3

Hush had long since settled upon Haddonsell Grange.

The household was abed, save for Penelope waiting alone in her comfortable sitting-room. This was *her* special corner of the Grange; the panelled walls were lined with shelves bearing her favourite books and music, painting and drawing materials, and hung with watercolours, oils and sketches from local artists.

Only the framed, fading pencil likeness of Colin Unsworth was by Penelope's own hand. She'd sketched it during their very last summer together. It stood on the corner of her desk, alongside Lydia's letter, the ink-well, sand-caster and tray of pens.

It was past midnight before Penelope heard the Grange's heavy front door opening. Hurrying into the tiled hallway, she confronted Adam as he was crossing the threshold.

'You're home at last!' she exclaimed in a low voice, mindful of disturbing the slumbering household. 'I've been waiting for you!'

'What's happened?' demanded Adam, shrugging off his hat and coat and tossing them aside. 'Is it Father?'

'No. No, Father's had quite a good day and is sleeping easy,' reassured Penelope at once. 'I've waited up because I must speak with you — '

'Whatever it is will have to wait,' he interrupted dismissively, striding past her to the broad staircase. 'It's been a long and wearisome day, and I've endured a thoroughly disappointing night when the cards were cruelly against me — I'm for my bed!'

'This *won't* wait!'

The light but firm touch of her hand upon his arm arrested Adam, and Penelope's grave, determined eyes met his steadily. 'It concerns your bailiff's behaviour toward the Macgregors. We can't talk out here.'

Quietly closing the sitting-room door behind them, Penelope considered her younger brother sceptically as he pulled her desk chair sideways and sank heavily into it, carelessly leaning an arm across the desk's surface and scattering her writing-tablet, pens and letters.

'Have you been drinking?'

'I've dined at my club and it does have a splendid cellar,' Adam replied, suddenly looking every inch the defiant, rebellious youth he'd been before Father packed him off to India. 'However, I own this evening their claret was exceptionally fine!'

'Whatever it was,' snapped Penelope, 'you've clearly imbibed far more than is good for you.

'Perhaps if you spent less time at your club and a deal more overseeing your bailiff, he would not have taken it upon himself to accuse the Macgregor sisters of trespass and order them from our land . . . ' went on Penelope, briskly relating everything Mathilda Macgregor had told her.

'I'd completely forgotten the Macgregors went to the priory,' remarked Adam soberly. 'I wasn't aware Gerrard had been out there, either.'

'That hardly surprises me, however what *reason* has he for going to the ruins? And who on earth is this armed fisherman?'

'I've no idea of the fisherman's identity,' responded Adam with a shrug. 'As for why Gerrard was at the priory — he's Haddonsell's bailiff, Pen! Overseeing the Whitlock estate — including the priory ruins — is his responsibility. Given that Gerrard's new to the situation, how could he possibly know the Macgregors have permission to trespass?

'Surely the man would have been negligent in his duties had he *not* evicted the party from our land!'

Penelope held her tongue, frustration and concern deepening. Adam would not hear a word said against Gerrard! Plainly, it would serve no purpose expressing her fears and suspicions of the bailiff's malign influence over her brother.

'Although no real harm was done and Gerrard certainly did not exceed his authority,' continued Adam evenly, 'I wholly understand how upsetting the affair was for the Macgregor girls. Profound apologies and amends must be made! You need worry your head not a moment longer, Pen. I'll call at The Bell and set all to rights on the morrow. Now, I'm going to my bed — I intend sleeping until I wake!'

Rising from Penelope's desk, Adam's gaze fell upon Lydia Unsworth's letter and picking up the page, he glanced over the hastily-penned lines.

'So Lydia's coming to visit, is she?' he mused, grinning across at Penelope. 'You know, before I sailed to India I was hopelessly in love with your friend Lydia.

'Of course, I was very young. Still too much a boy for her then,' Adam strode from the sitting-room, casting a wry backward glance at his sister.

'It'll be good seeing old Lydia again!'

★ ★ ★

'Are you coming with us?' exclaimed Amaryllis in astonishment when, wearing her best bonnet and cape, Dorcas appeared in the doorway of the slope-ceilinged bedroom her younger sisters shared. 'You haven't been to the ruins since we were children!'

'Well, I'm going today!' declared Dorcas airily, wandering in. Surveying her reflection in the freckled looking-glass upon the dresser, she tweaked the brim of her bonnet into a more becoming angle. 'It was most handsome of Adam — *Mr Whitlock* — to call and offer such humble apologies for what occurred. His insistence not only in accompanying us, but also in providing transport and a winter picnic, is exceedingly generous.'

Amaryllis was unimpressed. '*He's* the only reason you're going, isn't he?'

'What if he is?' returned Dorcas, glancing coldly at her sister. 'You're a sour lemon sometimes, Am.'

Amaryllis turned around from braiding Betsy's hair, nodding to Dorcas's modish footwear. 'You'll spoil your best shoes.'

'I shall take care not to,' she snapped, moving across to the low window and perching on the linen chest there. 'I'm *not* about to wear ugly great clodhoppers like those awful boots you have on!'

Securing Betsy's braids with two neat bows, Amaryllis smiled at the little girl. 'You're done! Mr Whitlock will be here soon, pet. Are you and Flossie ready?'

'Nearly,' Betsy scrambled down from the high bed onto her knees beside Flossie on the rag-rug, and began gently brushing the dog's silky white fur. 'I wish *Noah* was coming with us, Ammie!'

'Yes, it's a shame,' agreed Amaryllis, methodically gathering mittens and scarves from the tallboy. 'But Noah's away with the packet.'

'He'll be back tomorrow,' persisted Betsy. 'Can't we wait until tomorrow when Noah gets back? He'd take us in the mill waggon and we could all go for the Christmassy things and have our picnic together, just like always!'

'Mr Whitlock has organised everything for today,' replied Amaryllis. 'It's kind of him, Bets, and I'm sure we'll have a grand — '

'Adam's here!' cried Dorcas excitedly, peering through the small-paned window. A robust waggon drawn by a pair of sturdy horses was turning into The Bell's cobbled yard. 'And Am — he has your Simon with him!'

'He's *not* my Simon!' mumbled Amaryllis, vexed at the hot colour she could feel flooding her face.

'Not for the want of *wishing* he was, is it?' Dorcas retorted archly, sweeping from the sisters' bedroom. 'You've been making cow-eyes at Simon Baldwin for years, Am — perhaps one day he'll start noticing you!'

Although dull and overcast, the weather was dry with little wind and not particularly cold for the season, so they'd spent a pleasant day in Priory Woods, gathering Advent evergreens and choosing the yule log.

Adam Whitlock had provided an abundance of delicious food and when the party settled at the foot of St. Agnes Falls for their picnic, unexpected shafts of bright wintry sun glimmered down between bare branches to warm them as they ate. Well-fed and more than a little weary, eventually they had to start packing up, if they were to reach home in daylight.

'Does Flossie want a drink before we set off?' asked Amaryllis, bringing a bowl of water to where Betsy and the little dog were scattering crumbs for waiting robins and blackbirds. 'Had a nice day, Bets?'

She nodded, adding with a sigh, 'But

it's not the same without Noah.'

Amaryllis smiled, ruffling the little girl's hair. Betsy was right. Although it *had* been an enjoyable day, somehow it hadn't felt nearly as merry and festive as usual. Like Betsy, Amaryllis had missed Noah Pendleton's cheery presence — but spending a whole day with Simon was wonderful!

However, she'd been rather surprised to see that he and Adam Whitlock were such firm friends, and during the drive back to The Bell asked Simon how that was.

'Oh, we were at school together!' laughed Simon, his arm slipping along the seat-back and around her shoulders. 'Hadn't seen each other for years, until quite recently.

'We met across a card table in Liverpool — disastrous experience for us both,' he grimaced, shaking his head good-humouredly. 'While drowning our sorrows afterwards, we got talking and found we have quite a few common interests and ambitions.

'Adam Whitlock is a *very* useful friend to have!'

* * *

The York-bound coach coming apace from the direction of The Bell rattled past Kit Chesterton as he was riding from Akenside and down along the coast towards Macgregor's Cove.

Turning into the inn's cobbled yard, he saw Sandy and Iain grappling with a mighty gnarled log — and from where Kit was sitting, the huge yule log was clearly getting the best of the contest. Nearby, Mrs Macgregor was shaking her head in exasperation, while Betsy watched wide-eyed, perched on the corner of the stone horse trough with Flossie at her side.

Hurriedly leading Patch into the stable and removing her saddle and bridle, Kit left Betsy rubbing down the piebald mare while he sprinted out into the yard and joined the fray.

When the yule log was finally

manoeuvred into The Bell's great hearth and kindling nicely, the three men gathered around admiring their handiwork.

'We did a good job there, y'know,' pondered Iain, gazing from the log to Sandy and Kit and back to the log again.

'You did,' agreed Ethel Macgregor crisply, coming behind them. 'But we've no time for standing gawping.

'You're tall, Mr Chesterton,' she said, looking up at Kit. 'You might want to lend Am a hand. Even on tiptoe, she's hard-put to reach.'

Kit joined Amaryllis at one of the inn's big bay windows, where she was balancing precariously on a three-legged stool, assorted evergreens spilling from her arms.

'Does it sit along the top of the window?' he asked, taking the inter-twined holly, ivy and laurel from her. 'On this little ledge?'

'Yes, and try twisting it as you go so it makes a nice thick garland — oh, that looks lovely!' she exclaimed. 'There'll be pine cones going up there too — if Flossie leaves us any!'

Kit followed the direction of Amaryllis's glance to the chimney corner, where Betsy was sorting through a heap of pine cones. Even as Kit watched, Flossie rummaged amongst the cones, choosing one and tossing it into the air several times before catching it and dashing from sight.

'She likes hiding them,' laughed Amaryllis, as she and Kit moved along to the next window. 'This must be very different from your Christmas preparations in Jamaica, Mr Chesterton!'

'Although I *do* have some hazy memories of Christmas at home when I was a small boy, I've actually spent most in England.'

'How so?' she handed up another bundle of greenery.

'My brother Geoffrey and I went away to school when we were quite young,' replied Kit, stepping back to ensure the garland lay evenly. 'We grew up here.'

'Does your brother live in England too?'

Kit shook his head. 'After school, he returned to Jamaica. But I'd developed a keen interest in engineering, and begged my father to allow me to stay in England. Very reluctantly, Papa agreed and I've been fortunate in my opportunities . . . so here I am!'

★   ★   ★

The inn was bedecked for Christmastide, fragrant with rosemary and pine, and Sandy was helping Betsy light the festive Nicholas candles in their shining sconces when Ethel hurried through from the inn-house.

'Supper's ready — I'm dishing-up, so don't dally!' she announced and, turning back into the passageway, looked across at Kit, who was already on the stairs to his room. 'I've set a place for you, Mr Chesterton — you'll join us for supper, won't you?'

'It's kind — ' he began, reluctant to intrude upon the family.

'Come along through, lad,' chipped in Sandy warmly, clapping Kit on the shoulder. 'You're more than welcome at our table!'

★ ★ ★

. . . and progress on the Akenside Cut continues, penned Kit, seated at the writing table in his rooms at The Bell.

Despite it being almost noon, the wintry day was dark and gloomy; the candle he'd lit cast a flickering light across his letter, and upon the carved wooden St. Christopher.

Since sailing from Jamaica months earlier, Kit had carried Marietta's keepsake in his waistcoat pocket and now, as he wrote home to his elder brother, it lay at the corner of his page.

You'll see from my address I've removed from lodgings in Akenside and taken up residence at The Bell, a cliff-top inn overlooking Macgregor's Cove.

Yes, Geoff — the Macgregor's Cove oft mentioned in Alexander's letters to Marietta!

Alexander — Sandy — Macgregor is innkeeper. I believe Sandy is Marietta's Alexander — and my father. He lives here with his wife and three daughters.

Although The Bell is a busy inn with many travellers overnighting or staying a day or two, I am their only lodger. I find myself drawn into their daily activities and am coming to know and like the Macgregors very well — yet am I not somehow deceiving them? Taking advantage of their kindness and welcome?

Suppose I speak out and Sandy owns to being my father — what then the consequences for he and his family?

Oft times, I begin to believe I should remain silent, quit my rooms at The Bell and leave Macgregors Cove . . .

Kit wrote a while longer before sanding and sealing his letter. Deep in thought, he snuffed the candle, reached for his coat and hat and strode from his rooms onto the landing.

Amaryllis was hurrying upstairs carrying her basket of brushes, polishing cloths, beeswax and vinegar. She greeted him with her usual friendly smile.

Turning into Kit's rooms, Amaryllis set down her basket and even in the poor light, straight away spotted something lying on the floor beneath the writing table. Stooping, she retrieved a carved St. Christopher — and gasped in astonishment.

It was *Pa's*! But how?

'You've found it!'

Amaryllis spun around as Kit rushed into the room.

'Thank goodness!' he went on, coming forward to receive the medallion. 'I was in the stable saddling Patch before I realised it wasn't in my pocket!'

'It's *yours*?' she queried uncertainly. 'How — how did you come by this, Mr Chesterton?'

'It's . . . it's a family heirloom, I suppose,' Kit replied, taking the St. Christopher from her and gently folding his hand about it before returning the keepsake to his waistcoat pocket. 'Thank you for finding it, Miss Amaryllis. I couldn't bear to lose this,' he hesitated, adding with a small smile. 'It belonged to my — to my *mother*.'

★   ★   ★

During a lull between chores and coaches coming in, Amaryllis squeezed into her father's shed. It was crammed with all manner of tools and objects Pa refused to throw away because one day they were sure to come in handy. Rummaging amongst the dusty, cobwebbed shelves, Amaryllis finally unearthed a battered old tobacco tin.

She hadn't set eyes on it since she was a little girl, and had been in here with Pa while he was looking for something. Opening the tobacco tin, he'd tipped it upside down, spilling out a heap of long-forgotten odds and ends — amongst them a small St. Christopher. Fashioned from wood, it was very unusual — and quite unlike anything Amaryllis had ever seen.

She remembered picking it up, taking it to the light so she might better see the primitive carving, and asking Pa about it. As far as Amaryllis could recall, he'd replied that the medallion was a souvenir brought home from his Navy days, and he'd put it back into the tobacco tin.

Now, Amaryllis held the St. Christopher to the light exactly as she had all those years ago. It really was distinctive! Surely this, and the keepsake belonging to Mr Chesterton's late mother, *must* have been carved by the same hand?

★ ★ ★

Amidst a flurry of dry, powdery snowflakes — the first of winter — Lydia Unsworth arrived at Haddonsell Grange.

Penelope and Dorothy were on the front steps with Kit, who was about to take his leave, when the Unsworths' carriage laden with corded trunks, hat-boxes and an assortment of other luggage bowled up the beech drive. Accompanied by her lady's maid and abigail, Lydia duly disembarked, her appraising gaze immediately sweeping Kit Chesterton.

Penelope made the introductions before Kit rode away, and he was barely from earshot when Lydia widened her expressive eyes, staring at her friend.

'*Who* is that tall, dark and fiendishly handsome man?' she demanded eagerly, linking her arm through Penelope's as they started up the steps and indoors. 'Wherever did you find him?'

'I didn't!' Shaking her head, Penelope patiently explained. 'Kit — Mr Chesterton — is involved with Father's canal-building and has become a family friend.'

'Tell *that* to the pixies,' hissed Lydia,

eyeing her girlhood pal mischievously. 'There were so many sparks flying between you and your Mr Kit Chesterton, mine eyes were fair *dazzled* by their brilliance!'

★ ★ ★

Penelope's sitting-room was at the rear of the old house, overlooking Elias's flower gardens and bee hives. Draping a paisley shawl about her head and shoulders, she went through the French windows and across the terrace down into the garden.

There was scarcely a breath of wind now. Delicate snowflakes were floating from the late afternoon sky, settling upon her shawl and the dark earth for barely a moment before they melted and were gone. Penelope moved about the quiet garden, seeking out a handful of remaining hardy flowers to fashion into a posy for her father's room.

She hadn't yet discovered what had brought Lydia to Haddonsell with such urgency, for upon arrival Lydia went directly to her rooms to rest after the lengthy journey from Skilbeck. However it wasn't Lydia Unsworth who was presently occupying Penelope's thoughts. It was Kit.

He was worrying about something, of that she was convinced. Were there perhaps problems at the Akenside Cut that were preying on his mind?

'There you are!'

Lydia appeared at the French windows. 'Whatever are you doing out in the snow?'

* * *

'Thank you for giving me refuge,' she sighed, when they were ensconced in the seclusion of the sitting-room. 'I couldn't have borne being at Skilbeck another day!'

'You're as family, Lyddie,' responded Penelope warmly. 'We're very glad you've come!'

'You're doubtless wondering what

dreadful circumstance has driven me from my home.' Rising from the fireside sofa, she paced the comfortable room, too agitated to be still.

At the writing table, Lydia's gaze lingered upon the pencil likeness of her brother, and she touched a fingertip to its simple frame.

'How different everything would be if Colin had lived!' she exclaimed softly. 'You and he would be happily married with a hoard of small children, while I . . . I would be free to continue living my life and conducting my affairs as *I* choose — not as family duty dictates!'

'Whatever's happened?' queried Penelope anxiously, startled by Lydia's vehemence. 'How may I help?'

'Short of waving a magic wand and making the animosity between my father and his nephew disappear,' returned Lydia bitterly, 'there's nothing that will set this catastrophe to right!

'It's so *unfair*, Penny!' she railed, knotting and unknotting her fingers as she prowled the room. 'After Colin died, Papa named his only nephew as heir to the Unsworth estate. Everything was fine, until recently. They argued violently and are now estranged.

'Papa's cut my cousin from his will, and he's insisting I marry without delay. I feel so — so *helpless*!' Lydia declared in desperation, finally sitting down and meeting Penelope's eyes. 'Once I'm wed, a husband will control *my* fortune — indeed, my whole life! And since I am Papa's only surviving child, in time this husband will also come into the entire Unsworth estate!'

'Oh, Lyddie . . . ' Deeply troubled by her dearest friend's distress, Penelope put her arms about Lydia's trembling shoulders, seeking to comfort and reassure her, yet keenly aware there really was nothing she *could* say or do.

'I'm about to be forced into an arranged marriage with whomever my father deems a suitable candidate to inherit and manage the estate,' declared Lydia slowly, striving to regain her composure. 'And I'm utterly powerless to prevent it. Unless — I must find an acceptable husband with great haste, Penny!' she declared, resolve sparking in her intelligent hazel eyes. 'Before Papa finds one for me!'

★   ★   ★

'She's always been a very bright little girl,' Amaryllis was saying while she walked home from St. Agnes. Kit Chesterton was at her side, leading Patch and carrying Amaryllis's heavy basket of provisions together with an armful of books. 'Great Aunt taught her to read long before she started school, so Betsy's always loved reading!'

'I've noticed that!' smiled Kit, glancing at the books. 'She has a good selection here. Are they from Miss Macgregor's shop?'

Amaryllis nodded. 'After Betsy's illness, she couldn't go back to school, so Great Aunt began teaching her at home. She's very well-educated — Great Aunt, that is. When she was young, she had lessons alongside her brothers and was by far the cleverest. One of her brothers became a college professor. Great Aunt had ambitions to do the same, but of course wasn't allowed — '

They had, by this time, reached The Bell; Amaryllis broke off in surprise, seeing Simon Baldwin emerging from the inn and striding toward them.

'I've been here forever!' he exclaimed amiably, his glance darting briefly from Amaryllis to her companion, before returning to Amaryllis and the becoming blush colouring her cheeks. 'Where is everybody? Only your father, the hired hand and that old woman serving meals are about!'

'Ma, Betsy, Great Aunt and I have been in church arranging evergreens for Sunday — I've no idea where Dorcas might be,' she replied distractedly. 'I'm so sorry I wasn't here, Simon! I wasn't expecting you today. I thought you were going to Castlebridge.'

'My business there was speedily

concluded, and I'm presently away down to Liverpool,' he answered. Curtly passing the time of day with Kit Chesterton, he offered his arm to Amaryllis and led her aside. 'You'll excuse us, sir?'

'Of course,' responded Kit. He saw Amaryllis looking to the basket and books he still carried, and added with a smile, 'When I've tended Patch, I'll take these inside, Miss Amaryllis.'

Nodding her thanks, Amaryllis returned his smile but was immediately aware of Simon drawing her nearer, his head bowed so his lips were against her ear.

'You do realise,' he began in a low voice, 'that practically every time I come here — unexpected or otherwise — you're together with the Chesterton fellow?

'I don't like seeing you in cahoots with that stranger,' he concluded. 'Chesterton's far too old for you to be stepping out with him, anyway.'

'*Stepping out?*' echoed Amaryllis,

aghast. Glancing sidelong at Simon, she couldn't tell if he were teasing her or actually in earnest. 'I was walking from St. Agnes when I met Mr Chesterton riding from Akenside,' she explained briskly. 'He kindly carried my parcels and accompanied me home. Mr Chesterton's a *very* considerate gentleman!'

'Hmm, if you say so.' He laughed softly, drawing her nearer still. 'A man's entitled to be jealous about his sweetheart, is he not?'

Amaryllis gasped, looking up sharply, and suddenly her face was close to Simon's own. Her heart was thumping and she could scarce breathe.

Since childhood they'd been friends, never anything more, and yet — and yet — Simon was jealous! He'd called her his *sweetheart*! He really *must* care for her.

Tentatively turning toward him, she drew breath to speak. No words came, but her eyes met his. And in that moment, Amaryllis knew Simon Baldwin was about to kiss her.

★ ★ ★

During the hours after Simon left for Liverpool, Amaryllis hugged a new-found happiness, daydreaming through her mundane chores at The Bell.

It had been a long and eventful day, yet that night up in the room she and Betsy shared at the top of the inn-house, Amaryllis remained wide awake. Beside her in the high bed, Betsy slept soundly, with Flossie curled up in the hollow of her knees, also fast asleep.

The dog stirred when Amaryllis slipped from bed, looking up and yawning before settling her head onto her paws, and sleeping once more.

Padding barefoot across the room, Amaryllis took her shawl and went to the window, sitting on the linen chest. Swathed in the woollen shawl, she leaned upon the window's ledge and cupping her chin into her hand, gazed up into the ink-black sky; there was no moon this chill December night, and only the sparsest scattering of pale stars pierced the darkness.

Amaryllis noticed neither the dark nor the cold. Her thoughts and her heart were filled with Simon Baldwin, and her longing to see him again tomorrow when he returned from Liverpool.

★   ★   ★

That same moonless night, some eight miles north of Macgregor's Cove, a fore-and-aft rigged vessel showing no lights lay at anchor broadside to the ragged coastline.

On the beach, Haddonsell Grange's bailiff and the armed Manx fisherman, who went by the name of Killip, stood watching row-boats heavy with contraband edging into the shallows. A half-score of shadowy figures waded out to meet them, hauling the cargo ashore and noiselessly loading casks, barrels, chests, boxes and jars onto a train of docile pack-ponies waiting patiently by.

Straining and stumbling beneath the weight of their burdens, the ponies were duly led further along the shoreline, disappearing into a warren of caves and tunnels meandering deep beneath the priory ruins toward the storehouse vault. Gerrard and Killip were last to quit the beach and follow the train. Not a word had been spoken, for a voice would carry far on such a night.

Concealed amongst the plantation pines fringing the high ground above the beach, a lone horseman had observed the successful landing. Turning about, he rode soundlessly on the soft, sandy earth between the tall pines and away inland.

★ ★ ★

' . . . I can't think of anything else we need, can you?' remarked Penelope thoughtfully. She and her mother were in the sitting-room reading through the Christmas shopping list together.

The door opened and Lydia looked

in, warmly but elegantly clad for a trip aboard the packet, her flawless complexion glowing.

'We're setting off now!' she announced blithely, drawing on her gloves. 'It's a long journey and not the best of weather, but I couldn't possibly be staying out here on the coast without crossing the water to call upon my dear friends at New Brighton.

'It's awfully gallant of Adam to insist upon accompanying me aboard the packet!' beamed Lydia, glancing artfully at Penelope. 'And of course, I wish *you* an excellent day's shopping with Mr Chesterton, Penny!'

With that, Lydia Unsworth breezed from the sitting-room and was gone.

'Lyddie's my goddaughter and I love her dearly,' smiled Dorothy, shaking her head affectionately. 'But my word, she's like a whirlwind rushing through this old house!'

Penelope frowned slightly. While it was heartening to see Lydia in happier spirit, she couldn't help but be concerned.

From the day Lydia arrived at Haddon-sell, Adam had been extremely attentive — on occasion, even flirting — and Penelope felt anxious for her impulsive friend.

★   ★   ★

' . . . our first call in Castlebridge will be Quiggin's, the confectioner's,' smiled Penelope, consulting the shopping list while she and Kit were driving north toward the genteel Roman town. 'Mother has asked me to get a tin of Father's favourite Mabyn taffy as a special Christmas treat for him, and Father's asked me to buy a box of marzipan fruits for Mother because they're *her* favourites — ' she broke off, cross at her thoughtlessness.

Christmas would be a poignant time for Kit — especially this year — being so far from family and home. Touching her gloved hand to his sleeve, Penelope said as much, but Kit shook his head, briefly glancing at her before returning his attention to the narrow, winding road ahead.

'It isn't that.'

'Then what is it? I don't wish to pry,' she continued quietly. 'Something *is* weighing heavily upon your mind, Kit — and has been this past week. I know you sufficiently well to be certain of that. Can't you tell me — '

'You're not prying!' he interrupted fervently, meeting Penelope's eyes gravely. 'And you're the only person I *can* tell . . . '

She listened without saying a word while Kit poured out the whole story of finding Marietta's letters and the carved St. Christopher; of arriving in Macgregor's Cove on the day the yawl sank; of meeting Sandy Macgregor and his family; of coming to know and care for them . . .

'If Sandy were alone in the world, I wouldn't hesitate asking about Marietta,' he concluded as they jogged along the deserted wintry lanes. 'But Sandy has a wife and daughters. I don't want them hurt on my account.'

She nodded, understanding. Understanding, too, the turmoil of conflicted emotions Kit was struggling against.

He looked to her, and the anguish Penelope witnessed in his dark eyes tore into her.

'Whatever am I to do, Penny?'

'You believe Sandy Macgregor is your father,' she murmured at length, gently clasping Kit's cold hand within her own. 'Don't you owe him the chance to know his only son?'

★　★　★

He and Penelope had had a good day amongst the festive bustle of Castlebridge, and afterwards enjoyed a quiet supper together at Haddonsell Grange.

Penelope was very much in Kit's thoughts while he rode at an unhurried pace from the Grange to The Bell. It was late when he turned into the cobbled yard. Everywhere seemed silent and in darkness, save for the dim glow of a lantern over in the stables. Only

Sandy was still up and about, repairing a harness in the lantern's steady light.

He turned from his work when Kit led Patch into the stable, smiling up at the younger man. Kit thought he looked weary — and somehow very old. He'd never before noticed that about Sandy.

'Had a nice time at Castlebridge? Aye, it's a grand town right enough,' Sandy began cheerfully. 'Oh, Ethel's left a cold plate, in case you're hungry.

'The family's got used to you having supper with us at the inn-house,' he went on, adding a shade awkwardly, 'we missed you tonight when you were eating out!'

Feeling an unexpected rush of affection for his father, words suddenly failed Kit.

Reaching into his waistcoat pocket, he simply outstretched his hand toward Sandy Macgregor. Marietta's wooden keepsake lay on his palm.

'I — I believe this St. Christopher belonged to my mother . . . '

4

'*No!*'

Kit was shaken by the vehemence of Sandy Macgregor's response.

Shock and cold anger were flashing across the older man's eyes. Lunging forward to snatch the primitively-carved keepsake from Kit's hand, he suddenly recoiled as though burned.

'No . . . No, it *can't* be . . . ' he got out at length, his voice scarce more than a whisper. Standing stock-still with his head lowered, Sandy stared in confusion and sheer disbelief at the St. Christopher resting upon Kit's palm. 'However did you come by this?'

Drawing in a steadying breath, Kit explained. He left out no detail of how, earlier this year, he and Geoffrey had discovered the medallion and letters amongst Clara Chesterton's personal belongings at the family's home in

Florence, Jamaica, nor of what he had subsequently come to believe concerning his parentage.

'Aye, this is Marietta's right enough,' Sandy sighed, taking the keepsake. Slowly closing his fingers around it, he held it tight for a long moment before raising his face to meet Kit's searching gaze.

'Along the quayside at Jobert Town there's a tavern called the String o' Pearls,' he began simply. 'It was a low sort of place. And there was always an old man — locals said he'd been a famous pirate in his day — sitting in one corner making all manner of carved and scrimshawed curiosities.

'The day before my ship sailed from Jamaica, I went into the String o' Pearls and asked him to carve a couple of St. Christophers. One for me and one for Marietta. I gave it to her that last time I saw her — ' breaking off abruptly, Sandy turned from Kit and hurried from the stable.

'You get on with tending your horse

— I'll not be long!'

Carefully replacing the keepsake into his waistcoat pocket, Kit watched Sandy Macgregor walk across the cobbled yard and around from sight. He was rubbing down the piebald mare when Sandy returned.

'These past thirty-odd years I've kept this in my dad's old tobacco tin in the shed ... ' he muttered, hesitantly showing Kit a wooden medallion depicting the saint who protected travellers. 'It's a twin to yours — to *Marietta's*.'

'I've no idea how or why I came to be brought up as the Chesterton's son,' confided Kit evenly. 'And, of course, I don't know anything at all about Marietta. Who *is* she, Sandy? Will you tell me about her? How did you and she meet?'

'I'd gone to sea when I was twelve. Joined the Navy. I was nigh on eighteen when our ship put in to Jamaica for repairs — there was a big naval yard at Jobert Town — the crew was ashore

113

months while the work got done.

'There were church socials in the town every week, and one week I went along just for summat to do. That's when I met Marietta,' Sandy smiled sadly, recalling a day more than thirty-five years into the past. 'She was a seamstress in a shop that made fancy frocks and suchlike.'

'Was my mother *free*?' asked Kit bluntly.

'Aye, she was. And she was the daughter of a free-born Jamaican woman, too. Marietta's mother was housekeeper at one of the big houses on the ridge above Jobert Town. Her father was an English army officer. She didn't remember much about him. I think he'd long-since come back to England.

'I never thought Marietta would look twice at the likes of me,' he went on, sinking down onto an upturned pail. 'But we got to know each other, started walking out ... When my ship was ready to sail, I didn't want to leave her. I planned on lying low till after the ship sailed, then taking my chances ashore. It was the only time me and Marietta had a row!

'She wouldn't hear of me deserting. Said I'd be like a runaway, spend the rest of my life looking over my shoulder.'

'She must have feared for you,' frowned Kit soberly, his eyes downcast. 'Desertion from the King's Navy is a serious offence.'

'Too true,' grimaced Sandy. 'When a deserter gets caught, he's either flogged within an inch of his life or hanged from the yard-arm.'

'What did — '

Kit's question was drowned out by the bellowing of a driver's long-horn as the late coach from Liverpool rattled into the cobbled yard.

'I must see to 'em.' Sandy rose wearily to his feet, looking up at Kit before adding tentatively, 'I'm going out to Pendleton's Mill in a day or two. It's a long drive. It'd give us the chance to . . . If you want to come along, I mean?'

'I'd like that,' responded Kit warmly. 'There's much I want to ask you! A great deal I want to — to *know*.'

'Aye. Me and all, lad.' Sandy bobbed his head, darting a quick smile in Kit's direction before turning away. 'Me an' all!'

Remaining in the shadows of the lantern-lit stable, Kit Chesterton watched his father hurrying out into the yard to meet the stagecoach and welcome its passengers to The Bell.

⋆   ⋆   ⋆

'Mrs Macgregor and little Betsy called and left this for you!' announced Penelope with a broad smile, carrying a weighty stone flagon into her father's room. 'It comes with the Macgregor family's glad-tidings for the season!'

Elias Whitlock's gaunt face lit up. Every year he looked forward to the Macgregors' gift of mead!

'There's a fair few local folk use our honey for mead-making, but there's none makes better than Ethel Macgregor — and her special recipe Christmas mead is best of all!

'Put it there on the tall-boy where I can see it,' he went on. 'At least I'll be able to *look* at it — even if that quack Baldwin won't let me *drink* it!'

'Dr Baldwin's a fine physician,' chided Penelope, doing as she was bidden. 'His orders are for your own good!'

'Pah! He fusses. Still, come Christmas, I *might* manage a nip or two of Ethel's mead . . . ' Elias paused, going on ruefully. 'Y'know, Penny, this'll be the first time in better than forty years your mother and me won't be at the pottery giving out Goode's Day buns and boxes to our folk on Christmas Eve?'

'I know, Father . . . ' The sadness in his eyes caught at Penelope's heart. She understood how very much this tradition meant to her parents — and to all the workers at Whitlock's Pottery, too.

'It's Nora's day out, so Mother and I

are baking the buns today,' she said cheerfully, stooping to kiss his pale forehead before quitting the room. 'And I'll be sure to remind Adam about organising the boxes. Everything will be ready for giving out on Christmas Eve, just as always!'

★ ★ ★

'I'll leave the pair of you to it then,' remarked Haddonsell's cook, clamping on her warmest hat as she bustled back into the Grange's kitchen. 'Can I do anything before I go?'

'No, thanks, Nora,' smiled Dorothy Whitlock, already measuring out flour for the first batch of Goode's Day buns. 'Are you going into town?'

Nora Mumford shook her head. 'I'm going over to Akenside to see my niece.'

Penelope glanced up from chipping corners from the sugar-loaf. She remembered Joan Mumford well. 'Please do give Joan my regards, Nora; we were all sorry when she left the pottery.'

'No more than I was!' retorted Nora, adding grimly. 'I rue the day Joanie left Whitlock's, Miss Penny — and the day she wed that man of hers. He's a right bad lot.'

'If Joan ever wants to come back to the pottery,' Penelope ventured softly, 'we'll be very glad to have her!'

'I'll tell her, but . . . ' Nora shrugged in resignation, picking up her bag and making for the garden door.

After she'd gone, Dorothy began chopping the butter while Penelope set to mixing vine fruits, grated citrus peel, spices and sugar for the Goode's Day buns. However, speaking of Joan Mumford had brought thoughts of the pottery sharply to Penelope's mind and as she worked, memories both recent and from long ago flooded back.

From childhood, she'd looked forward to accompanying her father to the pottery once or twice every week. Learning how the goods were made, getting to know the folk who made them, understanding how Father managed the works

. . . When Elias fell ill, it'd meant the world to Penelope that he'd entrusted the management of Whitlock's to her — until Adam was able to return from India, of course.

Since then, she hadn't stepped within the pottery's gates. It wasn't her place to interfere, she knew that. But despite Penelope's knowledge and experience, Adam had never once sought her opinion or advice.

'I miss working at the pottery,' she declared unexpectedly, looking up from grating peel and meeting Dorothy's eyes. 'It was worthwhile work, Mother — and I was *good* at it!

'As a matter of fact,' reflected Penelope indignantly, 'I was *very* good at running Whitlock's!'

* * *

The first batch of Goode's Day buns were in the oven when Penelope heard Adam and Lydia returning from wherever it was they'd been together and, dusting her hands upon her apron, she hurried out into the hallway.

Lydia had already gone upstairs, but Penelope caught Adam as he was disappearing into the study.

'I must tell you — '

'Oh, no, Pen!' Adam groaned, turning around. 'What is it now? You've got *flour* on your face! Why are you rigged out like a servant?'

'Mother and I are baking the Goode's Day buns,' she replied and, seeing her brother's blank expression, explained. 'We distribute them to folk at the pottery along with their Christmas boxes.

'Actually, that's what I wanted to remind you about. Organising the Christmas boxes,' went on Penelope amiably. 'Would you like me to make a list of our workers' names for — '

'There'll be no Christmas boxes this or any other year,' replied Adam, striding into the study and leaving her in the doorway. 'It's an outdated custom and an unnecessary expense.

The workers already get a darn good wage out of us.'

'That's beside the point!' protested Penelope. 'The festive buns and boxes are our family's way of thanking everybody at the pottery for their hard work throughout the year, Adam!

'The tradition means such a lot to the pottery folk — and a great deal to Father and Mother, too! You simply *can't* — '

'I've made my decision. There's nothing more to be said,' interrupted Adam dismissively, reaching for a cut-crystal decanter on the mahogany sideboard.

'Whitlock's pottery and its affairs are *my* business, Pen — not yours!'

⋆   ⋆   ⋆

The horses' breath was steaming in the cold, crisp morning air and bright winter sunlight dazzled upon a crust of frost lying thick along the shoreline when Kit and Sandy Macgregor set off from The Bell.

This trip to collect the inn's flour was the first real opportunity the two men had had to be alone.

Kit had returned Sandy's letters to him. The little bundle of faded, dog-eared pages lay on the bench between them while the waggon trundled the steep track up-coast toward Pendleton's Mill.

'We were some weeks out of Jamaica when I fell from the rigging and got this,' Sandy was saying, indicating his maimed arm. 'Most shipboard sawbones would've taken it off, but the man we had reckoned it was worth trying to save the arm and patched me up.

'But I was taken real bad after. Burning up. Shivering cold. Out of my senses, most of the time,' he admitted. 'Soon as we put into port for fresh stores, they left me ashore at a mission-house. I was laid-up months before I'd come to enough to ask them to send a letter to Marietta and tell her where I was and what had happened to me.

'She wrote back, and told me about you. I hadn't even known Marietta was with child. If I'd known, I wouldn't have left her alone in Jobert Town like I did . . . ' His words petered out, and they drove on without speaking.

The only sounds were the cries of seagulls, the rasp of the horses' hooves as their shoes struck the hard ground, and the crunch of the waggon's wheels spinning and grating against deep ruts of frozen mud.

Sidelong, Kit considered his companion. Sandy's weathered features were taut, his gaze steadfast upon the icy cliff-top path winding away before them, an unlit clay pipe clamped between his teeth.

Kit's thoughts returned to the bundle of letters. He'd read their content only once, but well recalled that each of Sandy's letters to Marietta was filled with youthful declarations of love, of promises and of plans. So many plans! He'd come back to Jamaica as soon as ever he could. They'd get wed. He'd fetch her and their son home to Macgregor's Cove and they'd be together. But that hadn't happened, had it?

Kit broke the silence that had stretched for a mile and more of their journey. 'Did you ever return to Jamaica?'

'I was too late.' Sandy Macgregor's answer was quick and bitter. 'I got there too late.

'It was near two years since I'd sailed from Jobert Town before I got passage back. There was hardly anything left. It was horrible.' Horrible.' He shook his head, remembering. 'The town had been stricken with fever. They'd burned a lot of it to the ground to stop the fever spreading.

'Mass graves were everywhere. Some bore scraps of wood or stones scratched with names, but most of 'em were unmarked.' Sandy turned now, and Kit saw anguish in his eyes. 'I was told you and Marietta had perished: were dead and buried somewhere.'

Kit stared at Sandy. During the terror and chaos of an epidemic, it was small wonder if record-keeping and information were unreliable. The same thought struck both men.

But it was Kit who whispered, 'What if Marietta — my mother — what if she's *alive?*'

★ ★ ★

'There was no need for collecting me in the carriage, Simon!' smiled Amaryllis, when he was handing her down from the Baldwins' sedate vehicle. 'I would've been more than happy walking — and we *were* only coming in to St. Agnes!'

'There's little point possessing a carriage and driver unless you make use of them,' grinned Simon, offering his arm as they strolled along the crescent towards Prestcote's tea-shop. 'Actually, instead of bringing you for morning coffee and cake here at Miss P's, I'd far rather whisk you away to Castlebridge for a whole day's outing — *if* I could prise you from that blasted inn for more than an hour or two!'

'I have work to do,' she murmured apologetically, not explaining that Dorcas slipped away from The Bell to be with Adam Whitlock whenever fancy took, leaving her responsibilities to Amaryllis. It wasn't only because of the extra chores that Amaryllis felt reluctant to be long from the inn, though. She was increasingly worried about her father.

Pa hadn't seemed himself of late. He wasn't ailing or poorly, but something *was* troubling him.

'Here we are!'

Simon's cheerful voice broke into her thoughts, and Amaryllis gazed up at him, leaning a little closer against his shoulder as he ushered her into the genteel little tea-shop.

Miss Prestcote led them to a secluded table dressed with crisp white linen and adorned with a pretty posy-bowl of silken flowers. Simon ordered their coffee and cake and, leaning back in his chair, sat looking at Amaryllis without saying a word.

'I wish you wouldn't do that!' she exclaimed, annoyed at the blush colouring her cheeks.

'What would you have me do?' he demanded softly, reaching across the circular table to catch hold of her hand.

'I'm very glad you're spending more time up here now,' she began at length, keenly aware of his fingertips caressing the palm of her hand. 'When you first moved to your new job in Liverpool, you were away months and months!'

'The shipping company offering me this post at their head office was a considerable advancement in my career,' responded Simon soberly, his mood shifting. 'I wanted to fully establish my position there — and make the most of every opportunity it presents.'

'What is it you do, exactly?'

'Oh, ships, cargoes, manifests . . . You'd find my work deadly dull!'

'I'm sure I wouldn't!' Amaryllis

retorted. 'Because it's *your* work, Simon — and you enjoy doing it, don't you?'

'Hmm, I suppose I do!' He laughed, his eyes twinkling at her. 'Although when I was a boy, I wanted to be a dragoon! I'd seen soldiers from the garrison at Castlebridge with their red coats and shining swords. The notion of adventure, danger and excitement appealed to me. Still does, actually!

'Unfortunately, there's little profit to be made wearing the king's uniform,' concluded Simon, grinning broadly. 'So here I am in the shipping office!'

'Is there adventure, danger and excitement there?' laughed Amaryllis.

'You'd be surprised!' he returned, warming to the subject. 'Fortunes are made or lost in commerce and trade every day. The risks are huge, the dangers many. Seas, ships and the men who sail them are unpredictable.

'The world's riches flow back and forth along this very stretch of coast-line . . . '

Simon broke off, as Miss Prestcote brought their tray of fragrant, richly-blended coffee and the daintiest, most feather-light raspberry and almond cakes Amaryllis had ever seen or tasted.

★   ★   ★

Their morning together passed far too swiftly, and when Simon urged her to spend a little longer with him, Amaryllis was sorely tempted but reluctantly insisted upon returning to The Bell. The Carlisle-bound stagecoach was due, and Noah Pendleton would be bringing in the Manx packet with the tide. She'd be needed at the inn, especially if Dorcas had gone to meet up with Adam Whitlock again.

Actually, they got back rather later than Amaryllis had intended and passengers from the packet were already making their way into the inn. Amaryllis would have hastily alighted from the carriage, had not Simon arrested her.

'Wait — I have something for you!' he began exuberantly, retrieving an oblong parcel from its hiding place behind the carriage's side-cushions. 'An early Christmas gift. Aren't you going to open it?'

Amaryllis tugged at the string and sheets of thick brown paper fell away, revealing the soft folds of a silk dress-length.

'Oh, my!' breathed Amaryllis, her eyes wide. 'It's *beautiful*, Simon! Wherever did you get such finery?'

He shrugged. 'A big haberdashery in Liverpool. My mother and sisters are always singing its praises. It's on Bold Street.'

'Moseley's? I've heard about Moseley's of Bold Street!' she smoothed her fingertips across the shimmering silk. 'Great Aunt Macgregor says Moseley's is the best haberdashery in the whole of Lancashire — '

Amaryllis said nothing more, for Simon Baldwin had taken her into his arms.

★ ★ ★

Carrying the parcel carefully, Amaryllis sped up the steps and was about to enter The Bell when Noah Pendleton came out to meet her, his gaze upon the Baldwins' departing carriage.

'You've been out with Simon,' he commented.

Amaryllis nodded, her face becomingly flushed. 'We had morning coffee in St. Agnes and look — Simon gave me this silk for an early Christmas present! Isn't it beautiful?'

Noah drew a sharp breath. 'Wherever did *he* get something like that?'

'Moseley's,' she murmured, unable to tear her gaze from the rose-hued fabric. 'Simon bought it from Moseley's, the big haberdashery in Liverpool.'

'I'm sure he did,' remarked Noah drily, also eyeing the silk. 'Anyhow, I'd best be off. Are you coming to the carolling practice tonight?'

Without a word, Amaryllis shook her head and hurried away from him, the warmth of Simon Baldwin's parting kiss still lingering on her lips.

★   ★   ★

Ethel prided herself upon being a good knitter, however this particular pattern was not only testing her, it was slowing her down!

Although she'd begun the very day Mathilda Macgregor had unearthed the old family pattern and passed it on, Ethel knew it'd be nip-and-tuck completing the garment and getting it sewn-up and pressed in time. Needing to knit in secret wasn't helping either, but Ethel wanted it to be a surprise and had set her heart upon giving the gansey to Sandy at Christmas.

Catching the creak of approaching footsteps, Ethel hurriedly draped her shawl over her knitting as the back-parlour door opened.

'It's only you!' she exclaimed, casting aside the shawl and taking up her pins once more. 'There's fresh tea in the pot, if you want to help yourself.'

'My word, the front's coming along beautifully, isn't it?' admired Mathilda Macgregor, bringing her tea to the fireside and sitting across from Ethel, leaning closer to better admire the gansey's intricate pattern and variety of stitches.

'When I was a wee girl about Betsy's age,' she went on, settling into the rocking chair, 'I remember my grandmother telling me that that gansey pattern was unique to the Macgregor family and had been passed down through generations of womenfolk.

'I remember watching her knitting it, and I clearly remember my grandfather wearing it,' concluded Mathilda, sipping her tea. 'But since Grandfer's time, it's been forgotten — until now. Sandy's going to be delighted with his present, Ethel!'

'I've really struggled to get the tricky stitches right, but I've enjoyed making it,' she replied with satisfaction, her eyes upon her handiwork. 'Think I'll do another row before I go through to the inn and get the hot-pots into the oven. Have you finished lessons for today?'

'We have indeed! Betsy accurately completed the mathematics exercise well within the time I'd allowed,' responded Mathilda, adding with a smile, 'I've left her showing the map she drew of the Macgregors' journey from Scotland to your Mr Chesterton. He's paying great interest and asking sensible questions, which Betsy is happily answering and explaining!

'He seems a very kindly, thoughtful young man, doesn't he?'

'He has a good heart,' agreed Ethel, reluctantly putting away her knitting. 'Betsy doesn't take easily to strangers, but she's really warmed to Mr Chesterton — and with Betsy, it matters a lot that *Flossie* likes him too!'

★   ★   ★

'That afternoon when I first rode out to Macgregor's Cove . . . ' Kit recalled, while he and Sandy were splitting and stacking kindling in the barn-yard behind The Bell. He looked forward to these rare occasions of their spending time alone together, and liked helping Sandy around the inn. ' ... I half-expected to find you still living at the boatyard!'

'Iain and me were born and bred in the boatyard cottage, like generations of Macgregors before us,' replied Sandy, hefting another log onto the pile. 'If things'd turned out different, that's where I would've taken you and Marietta back to, until we could set up a home of our own.'

Kit paused for a moment, before asking, 'You didn't want to follow your forefathers into boatbuilding?'

'Iain had the will and the skill. I had nowt of either,' answered Sandy with a shrug. 'I never wanted to build boats, I wanted to *sail* 'em! I badgered our poor dad until he caved in and let me go to sea.'

'When I determined to stay in

England and become an engineer,' laughed Kit, 'I did exactly the same with *my* father — ' He broke off apologetically.

'Nay, lad. It'd be daft you and me watching our words,' put in Sandy earnestly. 'Mr Chesterton *was* your pa, and his wife your ma — for *they're* the folk who cared for you. Since you told me who you are, there's not a day gone by when I haven't thanked them for what they did.

'And I can't stop thinking about Marietta,' he confided, adding in a low voice, 'what if she *is* still living, Kit? Where's she been all these years? What's been happening to her? I just wish I *knew*!'

'I hadn't intended mentioning this, lest nothing comes of it,' ventured Kit after a moment. 'I've written to Tabby — Tabitha Warburton. She was with Mama fifty-odd years, since they were both young girls. Tabby's far more than a servant: she's part of the family and she and Mama were very close.

'Tabby helped raise Geoff and I. If anybody can shed light upon how and why I was taken in by the Chestertons, it will be Tabby. Perhaps she even *knows* Marietta!'

★　★　★

The opal brooch edged with pearls was small, yet it weighed very heavily in Penelope's purse as, with bowed head, she scurried through the sleety rain into St. Agnes.

Although she didn't have any money of her own, Penelope was determined to continue her family's custom of giving Christmas boxes to the pottery folk — and she very much hoped her little opal brooch would provide the means.

It was the only object with monetary value Penelope possessed, but she cherished it for a far greater reason. The brooch had been a present from Mother and Father upon her coming of age, and Penelope was heartsore at the very thought of parting with it.

Manoeuvring between the traffic of over-laden waggons, barrows, drays, carriages and riders coursing along the high street, Penelope was unaware of Kit Chesterton watering his horse at the trough over by the market cross. Amidst the clamour of voices, the rumble and clatter of wheels, and the ringing of hooves and boots upon slippery cobbles, she didn't hear Kit hailing her as she purposefully hurried toward the dimly-lit premises of Lionel Garber, watchmaker and goldsmith. Mr Garber also purchased and sold second-hand jewellery.

★ ★ ★

The heavy purse of coins was tucked away inside the top drawer of Penelope's writing desk. She was seated there, double-checking her Christmas box list to ensure no one at the pottery would be left out, when Lydia Unsworth bounded into the sitting-room brandishing a volume of poetry.

'What filthy weather!' she exclaimed, and with a deep sigh elegantly collapsed into one of the armchairs. 'Adam and I had planned upon driving over to Castlebridge, but I absolutely refused to set foot outdoors!

'He was terribly disappointed, of course,' Lydia beamed across at Penelope, her bright eyes sparkling. 'But I insisted. Told him I'd *far* rather curl up with my book and keep my dearest friend company!'

'Where is Adam?' enquired Penelope, slipping the list into the desk's drawer. She'd deliberately avoided her brother since their argument, and was determined he should neither discover nor thwart her intentions.

'I couldn't say,' murmured Lydia, gazing contentedly at her surroundings. 'This is such a beautifully *comfortable* room! Haddonsell is indeed a place where one can truly be oneself. I'm so enjoying my stay here!

'I'm also relishing Adam's gallant attentions,' she chortled, her eyes flashing mischievously. 'Is that terribly wicked of me? I'm almost four-and-thirty, and under no illusion he'd be wooing me with such ardour were it not for my fortune and the prospect of the Unsworth inheritance.

'However, if marry I must — I can imagine no more dashing, diverting or exciting husband than your handsome young brother, Penny!'

★   ★   ★

'That's a snow wind and no mistake,' grunted Iain Macgregor, while he and Sandy were clearing a blocked ditch in the quarter-field at back of The Bell. 'Come nightfall, we'll be snowed-up!'

'You've been saying that for days!' retorted Sandy, his face reddened from hours of strenuous work in the bitter cold. 'Have you *looked* at the sky? There's no snow up — '

'Ah, here's a welcome sight!' interrupted Iain, casting aside his spade as Ethel emerged swathed in shawls from the inn-house, heading their way with a large basket across her arm. 'By, summat smells grand!'

'Reckoned you'd be ready for your snap,' Ethel replied briskly, taking two billycans and muslin-wrapped bundles from the basket. ''Pasties are straight from t'oven, so get them eaten. They'll not stay hot long out here.'

'This is just the job, thanks,' said Sandy quietly, taking his share of the snap without meeting his wife's eyes. 'But you shouldn't have brought it out, Ethel. You could've given us a shout and we'd have come in.'

'What? And have you tramping muddy boots over my clean floors?' she exclaimed and, clutching the flapping shawls more tightly about her, strode back indoors.

'Ethel looks to be taking it well. What did she say?' asked Iain, moving close against the hedgerow and sheltering from the cutting wind before opening his tea-can. 'When you told her about Kit?'

'I — er — I . . . ' Sandy cleared his throat, following his brother into the hedgerow's windbreak and fixing his attention upon unwrapping the hot pasty. 'I haven't said anything to Ethel yet.'

'You haven't told her?' echoed Iain, aghast. 'What are you thinking on, man? She's your *wife!* You've got to tell her, Sandy!'

'I know that well enough, and I want to get it done and over with. But I can't find the right words, Iain — I can't fathom how to go about telling her summat like this,' confessed Sandy uneasily. 'Y'see, I've never so much as *mentioned* Marietta to Ethel — let alone told her the two of us had a boy!

'All them years ago, I'd wanted to fetch Marietta and Kit home with me. But when I come back on my own . . . Well, I never told anybody about them. Just couldn't. Not even you or Dad.

'It's different now, though,' he concluded, expelling a measured breath. 'I'm only waiting for a good time to talk to Ethel — '

'Oh, aye! A good time?' snorted Iain. 'And when's *that* going to come along, eh? Think back to what our Dad used to tell us when we were lads, Sandy.

'Dad always said putting off doing things as are hard to do only makes them harder. Ethel's alone up at the inn-house, isn't she? There'll be no better time,' he encouraged, punching his younger brother in the shoulder. 'Get yourself over there right now and do it — tell her Kit Chesterton is *your* son!'

5

'I've us dinner to make — and you've ditching to get back to.'

She and Sandy were standing facing one another across her little kitchen at the inn-house.

Stiff-backed, her gaze steady, Ethel had heard him out without saying a word. Now, you could hear a pin drop.

Turning away from Sandy and striding into the adjoining pantry, she methodically began gathering together potatoes, carrots, parsnip and onions. Only when Ethel felt the draught of icy air and heard the garden door shutting as he went outside again did she emerge with the heavy trug of vegetables across her arm. Sitting upon the three-legged hearth stool, she purposefully began peeling.

★   ★   ★

'My, that's a lazy wind — ' began Mathilda Macgregor, letting herself in at the garden door and immediately breaking off at sight of Ethel.

She was still at the fireside; a half-peeled potato in her motionless hands. With head bowed, Ethel sat dry-eyed and staring unseeing into the glowing logs. Her whole world and all she held dear had fallen down about her.

'Whatever is wrong?' Mathilda hurried to her side, resting a gentle hand upon Ethel's rigid shoulder. 'What's happened?'

While Mathilda busied herself brewing a restorative pot of camomile and honey tea, Ethel quietly confided everything Sandy had told her.

'As you well know, him and me weren't young when we met,' she reflected, sipping the dish of hot, soothing tea cupped within her cold hands. 'It wasn't until a good while later we started walking out. Longer still before he asked me to wed.

'I was far too old for fanciful, lovey-dovey notions,' Ethel went on. 'But I believed we were happy and had a blessed marriage. Yet every day of our life together he's kept the truth from me.

'All these years, I've been second-best to this Marietta woman. And she's given Sandy a *son*!'

* * *

'The grey or the blue, Betsy?' asked Amaryllis, turning around from the looking-glass in the back parlour and holding up two woollen mufflers. 'Which colour best matches my bonnet?'

'The blue,' Betsy was sitting cross-legged on the couch, with Flossie curled up beside her. 'Where's Simon taking you today?'

'I don't know. He didn't say,' beamed Amaryllis, considering her reflection and carefully arranging the soft woollen muffler. 'I really don't care where we go or what we do — I'm just looking

147

forward to being with him again!

'Simon's been so busy with his work, we haven't seen each other as often as we'd like.'

Betsy nodded, plainly unimpressed. 'Flossie and I, and Uncle Iain and Noah, are going out in the *Starfish* today — I wish you were coming sailing with us, Ammie!'

'I'll come another time, pet.' She smiled, dropping a quick kiss onto the little girl's forehead before gathering up her gloves and bag. 'You have a nice day!'

A while later, Amaryllis was still waiting for Simon to arrive. She stood at the window watching for him, vaguely aware of Uncle Iain and Noah Pendleton over in the cobbled yard putting finishing touches to a minor repair upon *Starfish*. Amaryllis saw Betsy and Flossie dash out to join the men as they were hefting the sturdy little boat onto a waggon, ready for pushing down onto the sands — then she spotted a boy hurtling into the yard, a message clutched in his hand.

Amaryllis was out and meeting him even before the lad got within yards of the inn-house. Rewarding him with a few coins from her purse, she hurriedly unfolded the sealed note and with sinking heart read its scant lines.

'*I've to ride to Castlebridge without delay. Adam Whitlock has put some lucrative business my way. My humblest apologies about today, dearest, you must surely know how I . . .*' Amaryllis blushed reading Simon's endearments.

'What does your letter say, Ammie?'

Amaryllis was startled from her thoughts.

'It — er — it's from Simon, pet,' she smiled ruefully. 'He isn't coming for me.'

'Then you can come sailing with us instead!'

'You're ready to set off,' replied Amaryllis, shaking her head. 'I'd need to change first and I don't want to keep you — '

'We'll wait,' chipped in Noah Pendleton, looking around from settling *Starfish* securely onto the waggon. 'We're in no hurry, Amaryllis.'

'Noah's right,' remarked Iain Macgregor, noticing the younger man's earnest, hopeful expression. 'And if you take my place aboard, I'll be able to help your pa in the cellar.

'Besides,' he went on brightly, stepping aside from the waggon. 'It's a grand day to be out on the water! Happen we'll not get another this side of spring. It'd be a shame to miss it. Isn't that right, Noah?'

★ ★ ★

Uncle Iain had been right — it *was* a grand day for sailing, reflected Amaryllis, raising her face to the pale rays of December sunlight and watching them dancing across the billowing waves.

She was sitting with Betsy and Flossie, hardly aware of Noah's deft handling of the little craft, nor of

Starfish sailing swiftly with the wind, away up the wild, craggy coastline until The Bell was far from sight. Amaryllis's thoughts were dwelling upon Simon Baldwin, and her disappointment at their not spending today together.

'We're coming a long way,' remarked Betsy contentedly, gazing beyond the beach up to the high ground, its dark pines silhouetted tall and stark against the cloudless winter sky. 'When are we going for our walk, Noah?'

'Right now!' He smiled over his shoulder at her. 'We'll put in anywhere along here.'

'You're going ashore *here?*' exclaimed Amaryllis, scanning the desolate beach with craggy grey cliffs rising above it. 'But it's not so great a distance from the priory ruins! You know what happened last time we — '

'We'll not trespass or walk anywhere near the ruins,' remarked Noah easily, taking *Starfish* into the shallows. 'And I very much doubt we'll bump into Bailiff Gerrard and his fisherman friend on the beach this afternoon!'

Once ashore, Betsy and Flossie streaked on ahead, skirting the water's edge. Amaryllis fell into step beside Noah, still uneasy at being here. She was watching Betsy and the little white dog playing their favourite game of looking for sand fairies, and hadn't noticed Noah striding away from her.

'Amaryllis — over here!' He was kneeling higher up the beach.

Keeping one eye on Betsy, she went to him — and saw a mass of boot and hoof tracks cut deep into the coarse, soft sand.

'Traders've sailed down-coast and landed contraband — since last high water, too,' declared Noah grimly. 'Somebody's running cargo up through the tunnels again, Am!'

★   ★   ★

Ethel was in the snug, polishing the small panes of the oblong window with cold water and vinegar, when Betsy

152

burst in with Flossie at her heels.

'Ma! Mr Chesterton is packing his bags! He's leaving us!'

Ethel sucked in a sharp breath, her heart suddenly beating fast. She prided herself upon being a practical, fair-minded woman. Since learning who Kit Chesterton was, she'd made it her business not to treat him a jot differently than before.

She and Sandy had not spoken of Marietta or Kit again. There was nothing more to say. Ethel's only concern now was protecting her daughters, and for her family's life to be happy and settled.

'Here, you carry on with this for me,' she said, handing the wet cloth and bowl to Betsy. 'I'll go up and see him.'

Ethel's mind was racing, her stomach churning as she slowly climbed the stairs toward Kit's corner rooms. It was her firm belief that what you can't change, you've to make the best of. There was no sense making a fuss. But this *must* be kept within the family!

Land sakes, if word ever got out, they'd never live down the shame and humiliation! Gossip and scandal spread like wildfire throughout the small town. She and her girls would be the butt of sniggers and tongue-wagging. They wouldn't be able to hold up their heads in St. Agnes ever again; what hope then of Dorcas and Amaryllis making good marriages? Or finding husbands at all?

Patting her hair into place and smoothing down her apron, Ethel turned along the landing to Kit's rooms and tapped lightly upon the open door.

'You've no cause to leave The Bell, Mr Chesterton,' she began, even as Kit looked up from packing and drew breath to speak. 'Things are as they are, but there's no reason we can't carry on as we were.

'Christmas is coming, and we'll keep the season as we always do. There'll be time enough afterwards for me to tell my girls who you are.

'I've said my piece and it's up to you what you do,' she finished, meeting

Kit's troubled eyes. 'You're welcome to stay here with us, and — and I hope you will.'

'Thank you, Mrs Macgregor,' he responded softly. 'If you're *sure* . . . Then, yes. Yes, I'd very much like to remain at The Bell.'

'Good. That's settled.' She bobbed her head. 'I'll be dishing up supper as soon as the carollers set off, so come down whenever you're ready.'

Ethel quit his rooms, suddenly a wee bit weak at the knees. There, it was said and done. Since Kit Chesterton arrived at the inn, she'd come to know him and taken a liking to him — but how queer it felt, knowing he was *Sandy's* son . . .

Downstairs, her three girls, together with Great Aunt Mathilda, Noah Pendleton and the rest of the St. Agnes carol-singers were milling about the inn: laughing and chattering; sipping the hot, fragrant apple and cinnamon cordial Sandy had brewed for them; lighting up their candle-jars and making ready for the evening ahead, when they would walk the length and breadth of the parish wassailing and collecting alms for the poor and needy.

'That young man of yours certainly has good taste!' beamed Ethel, admiring the lace Amaryllis was wearing at the collar of her dress. It'd been a present from the doctor's son, Simon Baldwin, and it warmed Ethel's heart that — all being well — both her eldest daughters looked set to marry well. 'It's beautiful, Am — I've never seen finer!'

Noah Pendleton also noticed the exquisite lace gathered softly about Amaryllis's neck and shoulders, and when the carollers were spilling out into the cold, clear night air he remarked drily, 'Another early Christmas gift from Simon Baldwin? Purchased like the silk from Moseley's of Bold Street, I daresay!'

★ ★ ★

'Miss Penny!' cried the old soldier in surprise, shuffling out from the cocky watchman's hut to meet them when they approached the gates of Whitlock's Pottery. 'Top o' the mornin' to you!'

'And the rest of the day to yourself, Mr Doyle!' responded Penelope as Kit drew the waggon to a standstill. 'How are you keeping? Is your rheumatiz any easier?'

'Ah, sure it could be worse,' replied John Doyle morosely; however Kit caught an unmistakeable twinkle in the elderly watchman's eyes. 'But not much!'

'This cold, damp weather won't be helping,' went on Penelope, dipping into her capacious bag. 'Father's sent a bottle to ease what ails you.'

'It's not liniment, I hope?' he queried suspiciously.

'I believe it's for your insides rather than your outs, Mr Doyle.' She placed a substantial flask of Irish whiskey into his hands. 'Mother and Father wish you glad tidings for Christmas!'

'The same to you, and your mammy and daddy!' he responded, adding somewhat grudgingly, 'Aye, and to that brother of yours, too, I suppose.'

Kit drove on through the gates into a cobbled yard. He'd never actually seen inside Whitlock's before. The pottery was built on an odd-shaped patch of land, and it seemed to him every square inch was crammed with workshops, sheds, huts, stores, and a long, three-storey house of sorts.

Men and boys with rolled-up shirt sleeves, clad in battered caps, long aprons and heavy boots were hurrying about their jobs, heads bowed and shoulders hunched against the keen wind. Women and girls darted across the yard from one workshop into another, their clogs ringing on the stone cobs. Drovers brought in a string of pack-horses bearing Dorset clay. An empty coal-dray trundled out. And dwarfing all of this were the great bottle-shaped brick ovens with their narrow-necked chimneys rising high into the murky winter's sky.

Although they were a landmark for

miles around, it wasn't until now — when Kit was close and craning his neck to look up at them — that he fully appreciated the immense skill of their construction; their sheer enormity.

Hearing Penelope's soft laughter, he turned to see her smiling at him. 'The bottle-kilns *are* huge, aren't they?

'I haven't been inside the pottery since Adam took over,' she went on soberly, gazing around. 'I'm thankful Adam has taken Lydia shopping in Castlebridge, so isn't here to cause unpleasantness and spoil our Christmas-giving.

'Thank you for coming with me today, Kit.'

Kit would have kissed her, had there not been a dozen and more people nearby; he had to be content with taking Penelope's gloved hand, feeling her leaning a little closer against him. She was wearing her opal brooch, and Kit was reminded of that rainy afternoon in St. Agnes when he'd bought it back from the watchmaker's shop, riding with the greatest haste over to Haddensell Grange to return the cherished keepsake to her.

'Where else would I be, Penny, but with you?' he whispered, going on after a moment, 'Besides, I'm looking forward to tasting one of those Goode's Day buns — so far, I've only been allowed to *see* them!'

'You'll need to wait until this afternoon!' she laughed, nodding to the stables away in the far corner. 'We'll unhitch the horses, then I'll show you how clay turns into cups and plates!'

⋆ ⋆ ⋆

It was long past noon when they emerged from the saggar-maker's shed to be hailed by a burly, red-faced man.

'You're a sight for sore eyes, Miss Penny!' he exclaimed, jerking his head toward their neatly-loaded waggon. 'I see you've not come empty-handed, neither!'

'It *is* the day before Christmas, Albert!' laughed Penelope, introducing

Kit to Albert Thwaite, the pottery overlooker. 'My parents are very sorry they can't be here doing the honours this afternoon.'

'To be honest, we weren't expecting Christmas boxes and such this year,' he returned bluntly. 'How're your da and mam getting on?'

'Father's still poorly but improving, and Mother's keeping well,' she replied with a smile. 'Albert, I hope we haven't been underfoot during our looking around?'

'Course not! Glad to see you here — both of you,' he added, with a polite nod to Kit. 'If you're going in t'house, you'll find Master's office pretty much as he left it. Young Mr Adam prefers the top room — *when* he's here, that is!'

* * *

'The painters, gilders and dippers work in here now; so do the flower-makers and the women and girls doing transferware. Our blue and white

161

Dutch-style patterns are especially popular,' explained Penelope, leading the way into the slightly crooked, three-storey, slate-roofed building. 'But when my parents first moved to Akenside, this was their home. I was born here. Father dug a garden for us at the back, and Mother planted her vegetables and herbs — although I doubt the soil was very good!

'This is Father's office.' She pushed open a door to the left of a broad, shallow staircase and they went inside.

Kit heard Penelope's sigh, glimpsed the sadness in her eyes as she moved slowly about the room. It felt chill, damp and forgotten. Everywhere was smothered by dust; the small square window soot-blackened and caked with grime. Cold, grey ashes spilled from the grate. A mildewed coat hung from the hat-rack, a pair of well-worn galoshes beneath it. Elias Whitlock's pipe rack and tobacco jar, his ink-stand, pens, papers, ledgers, letters and order-book were methodically arranged on the large, workmanlike desk.

'Albert was right. Nothing's been touched since Father — gracious!' Penelope's hand flew to her lips and she sank heavily into the straight-backed master's chair behind the desk, carefully taking up a sheaf of drawings. 'Our *Dorothy* designs — look, Kit!'

There was a selection of floral pencil sketches and watercolours, and Kit immediately recognised their style as being Penelope's own. There were a bundle of smaller drawings, too, depicting teapots, cups, milk jugs and plates in an assortment of shapes, each bearing the lightly-sketched outline of a floral pattern.

'Last year, Father asked me to design a special, hand-painted floral tea-set for Mother. It was to be a birthday surprise, and he — he called it the *Dorothy* tea-set,' Penelope murmured, a catch in her voice. 'He was really looking forward to our making it — '

Somewhere close by, a heavy brass bell clanged and Penelope broke off,

163

carefully rolling up the sketches and placing them into her bag. She glanced up at Kit, and in the room's dismal light he couldn't be certain there were not unshed tears shining in her eyes.

'That's the knocking-off bell. Whitlock's closes early the day before Christmas,' she said quietly, rising from behind the master's desk. 'It's time for the Goode's Day buns and Christmas boxes.'

★　★　★

Kit remained at Penelope's side as, amidst an abundance of high spirits, heartfelt good wishes for the master and missus's health and compliments of the festive season, everybody from the youngest mould-runner to the overlooker himself received their spiced Goode's Day buns and Christmas box of coins before hurrying homewards through the gathering dusk.

Driving out from Whitlock's cobbled yard, Kit drew to a standstill when Albert Thwaite flagged them down a short distance beyond the gateway.

'Beg pardon, sir — Miss Penny,' the overlooker began awkwardly. 'I know it's not my place, but if I don't speak out I'd be letting down the master, and all us who depend on t'pot-works to feed us families.'

'Of course you must tell me!' responded Penelope urgently, for Albert Thwaite was not a man to make mountains from molehills. 'Whatever's wrong, Albert?'

'Folk don't like your brother. Don't like him, don't trust him. He's hardly ever here and he knows nowt. Truth is, he dun't give a cuss about t'pottery, miss,' complained the overlooker grimly. 'You or the Master need to come back and take over before Mr Adam runs Whitlock's into the ground — and us workers' livelihoods with it!'

★ ★ ★

On the first morning of the New Year, Amaryllis stirred to see Betsy and

Flossie sitting up on the oak linen chest beneath the window. The little girl was breathing on the glass, using the sleeve of her flannel nightgown to rub a clear patch on the frosted pane and peering out at thick, softly drifting snowflakes.

Amaryllis closed her eyes again. Her head throbbed. She'd lain wakeful most of the night. Yesterday, Ma had taken she, Dorcas and Betsy aside, and told them Kit Chesterton was Pa's son.

★   ★   ★

It wasn't until that afternoon, after Betsy and Flossie came indoors from playing in the snow, that the three sisters settled down together in the back parlour.

While Betsy toasted her toes at the hearth, Amaryllis and Dorcas sat either side of the fire, sewing-baskets at their feet and mending on their laps, making the most of this opportunity to discuss Kit Chesterton. Betsy hadn't spoken. She'd curled up beside Flossie, her arm

166

about the dog's silky neck, watching her sisters and following their every word.

'I keep seeing poor Ma's face while she was telling us,' murmured Amaryllis, brushing a tear from her cheek with the back of her hand. 'That awful sadness in her eyes.'

'I'm furious with Pa!' blurted Dorcas bitterly, stabbing her needle into the torn seam of Betsy's calico smock. 'When Chesterton turned up at The Bell, Pa should have sent him away. This whole disaster could've been avoided if Pa had put his *proper* family first!'

'Ma must be so very hurt and unhappy,' reflected Amaryllis, her head bowed over the stocking-heel she was darning. 'Last night, all she could think about was comforting and reassuring us — but it's *Ma* who needs comfort!'

'If this scandal gets out, Am, our reputations will be ruined! Adam Whitlock won't marry me. Nor will anyone else of quality. I'll end my days here at The Bell — and so will you

— an old maid scrubbing floors and cleaning up after other people.

'If I lose Adam, I swear I'll *never* forgive Pa or Kit Chesterton!'

'Ma told us not to worry because everything would be alright, didn't she?' reasoned Amaryllis thoughtfully. 'And, well, I haven't heard even a cross word between Ma and Pa, have you? They've been doing their chores together as usual, so perhaps everything *will* be alright.'

'Hmm, and Ma *did* stress this news must be kept inside the family . . . As long as nobody else finds out, Pa having a happenchance offspring hardly matters, does it?' considered Dorcas, calmer now. 'Once the canal cut is finished, Kit Chesterton will leave Lancashire and we'll never have to see him again.

'Unlike *some* people who fell over themselves being friendly and making Chesterton feel at home,' she finished caustically, glaring at Amaryllis, 'I never took to him.'

'I did. I really *liked* Kit, and regarded him a friend,' confessed Amaryllis uncomfortably. 'But now . . . I've been avoiding him today. I can hardly bear seeing him, much less talking to him! I wish he'd never come to Macgregor's Cove — '

'You're mean and selfish — both of you!' Betsy rounded on them, her outburst shocking her older sisters into silence. 'Kit's mother died when he was a baby and he didn't know who he really was until this year.

'We're his *family*,' she declared stoutly, her blue eyes wide and earnest. 'Kit's our brother — the only brother we have — and *I* love him!'

★ ★ ★

'Dorcas — *Dorcas*!' Ethel scurried from the inn and across the back yard into the wash-house, where her eldest daughters were dollying a huge mound of bed linen. 'A groom from the Grange brought this for you!'

169

Pushing aside the heavy wooden dolly, Dorcas hastily dried her hands on her apron and rushed to open her letter.

'It's an invitation to a January ball at Haddonsell Grange!' Dorcas held out the card, then suddenly her excited face was stricken. 'I don't have a ballgown, Ma — whatever am I to *wear*?'

Ethel's cheeks were glowing with pride at reading her daughter's name on the impressive card, but already she was racking her brains about Dorcas's wardrobe.

'There isn't enough time for us to make a ballgown,' she began. 'But we'll sort something out. I'll get the *Lancashire Ladies' Journal* from Great Aunt, and we'll look at the fashion plates to find out what's modish for young ladies. Then we'll see what ideas we can borrow to make over your ivory muslin. It's the best material, and drapes well across the bodice. With a few changes and embellishments it'll be perfect.' Ethel hurried from the wash-house. 'Don't worry, Dorcas — Mr Adam won't be able to take his eyes from you!'

After she'd gone, Amaryllis considered Dorcas warily. They'd never been close, nor even got along particularly well, and she knew Dorcas would bitterly resent her interference. Nonetheless, Amaryllis felt compelled to warn her quick-tempered sister.

'Dorcas,' she said, pausing from vigorously dollying bed-sheets, 'about Adam Whitlock — '

'*What* about him?' demanded Dorcas crossly, glowering across the tubs of hot water.

'I saw him in St. Agnes. With a lady,' relayed Amaryllis. 'She was on his arm, Dorcas. They looked — well, *intimate*.'

To her amazement, Dorcas gave a short, derisive laugh.

'Am, you're priceless! Adam's told me all about her. Her name's Lydia. She's a spinster who's visiting the Grange. Adam's simply being chivalrous toward his sister's old friend.'

'I *know* what I saw,' persisted Amaryllis in a low voice. 'You need to be careful, Dorcas!'

'Are you going into town?' queried Sandy, spotting Ethel hurrying from the inn-house wearing her best hat and coat. 'I thought Am got the errands in St. Agnes yesterday?'

'So she did,' replied Ethel, tucking the *Lancashire Ladies Journal* more firmly beneath her arm. 'I'm off to the draper's.'

'There's no sense fussing about Dorcas's frock. Happen I should've said summat sooner,' he went on awkwardly, 'but I've been thinking, and I'll not let her go to that fancy do at the Grange.'

Ethel froze, glaring at him. Her lips compressed into a hard, thin line. When she did reply, her voice was very, very quiet. 'Why would that be, Sandy?'

'It'll be too grand by half, and filling the girl's head with such nonsense is asking for trouble,' he returned, trying to explain. 'There'll be plenty people at that do who'll look down their noses at

Dorcas because they'll know she dun't fit in there.'

'You're wrong!' retaliated Ethel, anger and frustration igniting deep within her. 'Haddonsell Grange is *exactly* the sort of place Dorcas belongs!'

'Listen, I like the Whitlocks and it was good of them to invite her — but them and their sort aren't our class,' he went on, patience rapidly wearing thin. 'No good'll come of Dorcas going up to the Grange and getting ideas above herself, Eth. Surely you must see that?'

'Why is it fitting for your *son* to be courting a Whitlock,' she lashed out, the simmering hurt, anger and resentment of recent weeks spontaneously boiling over, 'but our *daughter* isn't good enough to even attend a dance at their home?'

'That's not what I meant — '

'Adam Whitlock is the best prospect our girl will ever have,' cut in Ethel coldly, her fury spent as swiftly as it erupted. 'You aren't going to ruin her chances of making a fine marriage,

Sandy Macgregor — I'll *not* allow it!'

Only a week earlier, Adam Whitlock had decided something gay and lively was needed to brighten the drear January days and asked Lydia Unsworth if she'd be so gracious as to help organise a ball at Haddonsell Grange.

Never a woman to miss a diverting opportunity, Lydia threw herself into arranging musicians, singers, party games and refreshments for a grand ball the like of which old Haddonsell Grange had probably never seen.

'Everybody's certainly enjoying themselves!' remarked Kit on the night of the ball. He and Penelope had woven their way from the crowded floor and, along with other couples and clusters of chattering friends, were sitting listening to the music and watching the dancing. 'This really is quite a party!'

'Lydia arranged everything, but Adam drew up the guest list,' Penelope commented wryly, surveying numerous dancers and merrymakers who were becoming more exuberant with each passing hour. 'I don't know most of these people. Members of Adam's club in Castlebridge, I suppose. With their ladies.'

'Speaking of ladies, Adam's paying a deal of attention to Dorcas, isn't he?'

'Yes. I hadn't realised he and Miss Macgregor were so well acquainted.'

'Nor had I,' Kit replied, with another concerned glance at his sister. 'Has he actually danced with anyone else?'

'Not since the first dance, when he and Lydia opened the ball. Since then, Adam's been flirting outrageously with Miss Macgregor — and ignoring Lydia.'

'Perhaps Miss Unsworth hasn't noticed his lack of attention,' suggested Kit mildly, when Lydia swirled past them, beaming at her dashing, flaxen-haired partner and caught up in one of the new, daring dances from the continent.

'Oh, Lydia's never short of admirers!' laughed Penelope affectionately, watching her friend. 'Besides, she's more than a match for my brother — although he's far too arrogant to realise it.'

'You still haven't spoken to him about everything the pottery overlooker told us?'

She shook her head. 'I'm afraid if I tackle Adam about neglecting the pot-works, it'll cause trouble here at home. Father's looking better and brighter than he has in many months, Kit. I daren't risk setting back his recovery with worries about Whitlock's.

'Albert Thwaite is absolutely correct, though. Something must be done, and soon. I need to look after the pottery and safeguard its prosperity, *without* antagonising Adam or alarming my father — and I think I may have found a way of doing it!'

⋆ ⋆ ⋆

It was the wee small hours before the last of the revellers were finally borne away in their carriages, and quietude settled once more upon Haddonsell Grange.

176

Lydia had plumped for hot chocolate and retiring some while earlier. Penelope hadn't seen Adam for hours, and had no idea where he was. However, after Kit kissed her good-night and rode home to The Bell, instead of going up to her room, Penelope took her hot chocolate into her father's old study.

Since returning from India, Adam often used the large, old-fashioned room but hadn't made any changes to its furnishings. Although the fire was burning low by this late hour, Elias's study still felt comfortably warm. Penelope lit one of the lamps and went across to the window. The heavy velvet curtains had not been drawn closed, and she chose to leave them wide open. She sat there in the winged chair, sipping her chocolate and looking out into the frosty, moon-washed garden. Penelope had much to occupy her mind.

She knew not how long she sat before the study door opened and Adam stood on the threshold.

177

'What are *you* doing in here?'

'I was thinking.'

'How splendid.'

Shrugging off his elegant evening coat, he loosened the neck of his shirt and made for the mahogany sideboard with its selection of crystal decanters and glasses.

'Haven't you had enough of that tonight?'

'One can never have enough of fine old brandy.' He grinned over his shoulder at her. 'And I can assure you, this particular brandy is *very* old and exquisitely fine!'

'Your behaviour during the ball was reprehensible.'

'Oh, but surely you're mistaken!' He stretched out across one of the sofas. 'I was charming all night long — ask anybody.'

'From the moment Lydia arrived at the Grange, you've ardently courted her. Yet you spent this entire evening flirting openly with Miss Macgregor.

'It was a cruel, calculated ploy — at

the expense of both ladies,' concluded Penelope in disgust. 'Because it *is* Lydia you've set your sights upon, isn't it?'

Adam shrugged, rising to pour another brandy.

'Dorcas is a real beauty, Pen old girl, and I truly do care for her,' he sighed, shaking his head ruefully. 'If only *she* were the heiress with a fortune and legacy of old money!'

* * *

' . . . I'll fetch the horses, then we'll be on our way,' Simon Baldwin said as he and Amaryllis came down the worn stone steps from The Bell. With a sly glance back towards the bustling inn, he added, 'I'm looking forward to having you all to myself — even for a short while!'

He kissed her cheek before striding toward the stables. However, Amaryllis's gaze didn't follow Simon as it usually did. She'd caught sight of Kit Chesterton and Betsy down on the beach. They were collecting shells together — just as any elder brother and wee sister might.

Amaryllis watched them in dismay, deeply regretting her recent coldness toward Kit. She hadn't been fair to him. Or kind.

The tide was far out, leaving pools and seashells in its wake. With Flossie scampering at her side, Betsy was wandering ahead of Kit and Amaryllis saw the little girl stooping to pick up a shell. Swishing it clean of sand in the saltwater, she ran back to Kit, her happy little face upturned as she offered the shell for him to look at.

An unexpected lump came to Amaryllis's throat while she watched Kit and Betsy carefully examining the shell together. He knelt on the wet sand to match Betsy's height and they held the large buckie shell against their ears, listening for the sound of waves.

'*Kit!*' called Amaryllis impulsively, and hitching up her skirts she dashed down onto the shore.

Emerging from the stables with their horses, Simon was too far away to hear whatever was said, but he plainly saw Amaryllis gazing up at the man — *and* witnessed the embrace that followed.

'What the devil's going on, Am?' demanded Simon when, with face flushed and eyes shining, she ran up from the beach and joined him. 'I *saw* you — in his arms!'

'In his — ' she began incredulously, then laughed and scolded, ' — oh, Simon! Don't be so silly and cross — Kit's my *brother!* Besides, I wasn't exactly in *his* arms, because it was *I* who gave the hug — '

Amaryllis broke off, biting her tongue. But it was too late. The words could not be unsaid. Nor could she read the sudden expression flashing across Simon's handsome features.

'Simon — I shouldn't have told you about Kit!' she gasped. 'You won't breathe a word to anyone, will you?'

'Course not,' he responded at once, catching both Amaryllis's hands and drawing her close, while casting a quick sideways glance to the beach where Kit Chesterton was strolling with the child and the dog. 'You have my oath 'pon it, Am.'

★　★　★

'Your carriage is being brought around to the front door,' Penelope said, coming into her sitting-room where Lydia was waiting. She had only to put on her bonnet and gloves to be ready to leave Haddonsell Grange. 'Adam insists upon escorting you to Skilbeck.'

'Rather thought he might,' sighed Lydia, going on. 'I wish I weren't rushing off like this, Penny! But now Papa is lining up our dull, highly respected, landowning neighbour to be my husband, I feel I really must go back and face the situation.'

Penelope nodded sympathetically. The letter from Mr Unsworth was brief and stern, but not without affection. It arrived late last evening, and Lydia had immediately decided to return home.

'I wish I could do something to help you!'

'My dearest friend, you already have!' exclaimed Lydia earnestly. 'You gave me refuge when I was in deepest despair. I've thoroughly enjoyed my stay at Haddonsell and,' she paused, a spark of mischief suddenly lighting her eyes, 'Adam's passionate and persistent wooing did wonders for my flagging spirits!'

Penelope smiled, but her voice was solemn when she asked, 'Shall you be content with this neighbour your father's chosen for you?'

'Needs must, I suppose,' answered Lydia matter-of-factly. 'I can't recall a time when I didn't know Arthur Smedley. I believe he's liked — cared — for me for a considerable while.

'Mr Smedley will never set my heart racing as Adam does,' she owned frankly, 'but he's considerate and trustworthy, while Adam is selfish and utterly unscrupulous.

'At the ball, he flaunted that poor innkeeper's daughter to pique my jealousy,' continued Lydia briskly. 'I suspect he intends making an offer of marriage during our long journey to Skilbeck.

'I feel sorry for Dorcas Macgregor. She truly loves him, Penny — and your ruthless brother will break her heart!'

6

The Redcoats were taking their leave of
Sandy and Iain Macgregor when Kit
and Amaryllis turned from the lane,
and The Bell's cobbled yard came into
their sight.

'I don't believe I've seen soldiers at
the inn before,' remarked Kit, watching
as a final few words were exchanged
before the Macgregor brothers resumed
working on the stable door. 'Or in St.
Agnes either, come to think of it I've
never seen any myself,' commented
Amaryllis, glancing over her shoulder to
ensure Betsy and Flossie were not
lagging too far behind. 'But then again,
the garrison *is* miles away over at
Castlebridge.'

'It's within the castle itself, isn't it?
Along with the gaol and courts of law?'
he queried. 'I've visited the town a
couple of times with Penny. I haven't

seen the Roman ruins yet, but the castle is magnificent, isn't it?'

'I've never been to Castlebridge,' sighed Amaryllis, her face colouring a little as she added, 'but Simon's promised to take me soon! He goes there often to his club, and says it's an elegant town with excellent theatres, hotels, a concert hall, assembly rooms and an art gallery — '

They'd started into the yard and she broke off, beckoning Betsy to hurry before smiling across at Kit. 'Are you coming up to the inn-house for tea?'

'No, thanks.' He returned her smile, indicating the massive stable door lain flat on the cobbles. 'I'll see if I can do anything useful out here!'

Crossing the yard to where Sandy was on his knees beside the door, Kit took off his coat and hung it over the water pump.

'The old hinge couldn't be fixed, then?'

'Had to have a new one made.' Sandy glanced around from tightening home the screws securing a long hinge to the thick timber. 'There's some weight to this door, even with the three of us we'll have a devil of a job hanging it — '

'Did you see the Redcoats, Kit?' called Iain, emerging from the stone tool shed carrying a short ladder. 'They were asking after the smugglers running cargo up-coast!'

'Aye, and more's the pity,' chipped in Sandy, straightening up. 'It's plain they've no intelligence who the men are, *nor* who's behind them and giving the orders!'

'Y'see, Kit, them as are on the beach bringing the goods ashore and carrying it to safe-houses are only hired hands,' said Iain, warming to the subject. 'It's somebody high-up who organises it all, and even the runners themselves won't know who *he* is!'

'Hark at your uncle!' Sandy looked at Kit, but cocked his head in Iain's direction. 'The authority on free-traders and their paymasters!'

'I'm right though,' argued Iain,

propping the ladder against the stable wall. 'You think back to when we were lads, Sandy, when smuggling was not only rife up-coast, but right *here* in this cove!

'Didn't our dad always say it was the magistrate behind it? This was long before Elias Whitlock came to Haddon-sell and got posted magistrate, Kit — ' he put in by way of explanation. 'Nowt was ever proven, o'course, but Dad said the magistrate, many a local squire and other gentry were happily turning a blind eye to smuggling because *that's* where they were getting their brandy, 'baccy, tea, spices and all the rest — without having to pay duty on 'em!'

'Aye, that's true enough,' agreed Sandy soberly, 'and there were plenty of honest, decent folk who got threatened into keeping quiet. They lived in fear of what'd happen to them and their families if they spoke out about what they'd seen and heard.

'It took Elias Whitlock to crack down and rid this coast of smuggling — and I reckon now he's laid-up ill, somebody's seen their chance and started it up again.'

'Penny's told me a little of what she remembers about those early years when her father became magistrate,' remarked Kit quietly. 'She recalls them as being frightening times.'

'So they were, for the whole Whitlock family!' exclaimed Sandy. 'There were plenty of powerful folk along this coast and around the whole county who were profiting one way or t'other from contraband — and they were dead-set against Whitlock's efforts to stamp it out!

'His life was threatened and his home attacked by night, but Elias stood fast and wouldn't give up.'

'He had dangerous enemies with long arms,' nodded Iain. 'As Sandy said, even them as had no truck with smuggling were too afraid to stand with him — until the wrecking at Gibbet Point . . . '

'Great Aunt Mathilda told me about

the *Jupiter*,' Kit murmured grimly.

Scores of men were lost — murdered — when the merchantman *Jupiter* bound for Liverpool carrying a cargo of luxury goods was lured to her destruction by a wreckers' light high on Gibbet Point.

The young Macgregor brothers and their father had been first down on the beach, putting out boats and ropes to pluck or haul drowning men from the cauldron of churning black water and clear of the treacherous Gibbet rocks.

'I pray I never see another night like it,' mumbled Iain.

'Amen to that.'

The three men fell silent, and set to the troublesome task of hanging the stable's door.

★   ★   ★

It was late.

Noah Pendleton had brought in the Manx packet hours ago; the last coach of the night had been and gone long since. The passengers and travellers were fed, watered, and had either gone on their way continuing their journeys or been shown up to their rooms at The Bell.

In the stillness of near-midnight, the Macgregor brothers, Noah Pendleton and Kit Chesterton were seated in the window alcove, lingering over their ale and the game of bonesticks playing out across the table between them.

In the inn's big kitchen, Amaryllis, Ethel and Widow Watkins were putting away the newly-washed crockery, cleaning and tidying and making ready for a new day in the morning. Amaryllis was also watching over chocolate heating on the hob, but not for the first time that evening she glanced with increasing concern at her mother.

Ma looked worn-out, her thin face pale and drawn. She worked far too hard and besides, Amaryllis guessed these past weeks since finding out about Kit must've been very difficult for her.

'I'll finish in here,' she smiled, pouring the hot chocolate into large earthenware mugs. 'Why not take yours and go on up to bed, Ma — you too, Mrs Watkins!'

Ethel shook her head.

'I'm fine, Am. Besides, with Dorcas out with Mr Adam, everything's been left to you today.'

'There isn't much left to do,' persisted Amaryllis cheerfully, 'and I'm not tired at all tonight! I'm so excited about Simon's asking me to the theatre!'

'Me and my Archie went to a theatre once,' recalled Freda Watkins. 'It was about a young lass and lad who fell in love during olden times. They both died at the end. It were very sad.'

'I hope Simon and I see a happier play!' laughed Amaryllis, placing mugs into her mother and Mrs Watkins's hands. 'Away you both go. Sleep well!'

After Ethel had gone through to the inn-house and Widow Watkins climbed the back stairs to her rooms above the big kitchen, Amaryllis finished the remaining chores and fetched in fresh water for the morning, lest the pump freeze during the night, before following her mother into the inn-house.

Ethel had indeed retired, however Amaryllis didn't follow suit. Instead, she went along into the back parlour, lighting the lamp and taking the silk dress-length Simon had given her for Christmas from the sideboard drawer. Removing the material from its brown-paper wrappings, she carefully smoothed it out across the oval walnut table and stood back, considering.

Simon had told her they were attending the opening night of the new season at the Castlebridge Playhouse. That was still weeks away, so there would be enough time to make a dress from the silk — but was such a pale colour and sheer fabric suitable for the theatre? Her only experience of theatricals was the St. Agnes Players at the church hall.

'Amaryllis.'

She turned to see Noah Pendleton in the doorway.

'Your pa said it was all right for me to come through.'

'Of course!' she exclaimed with a smile. 'How did the bonesticks turn out?'

'It was Kit and I against your pa and Iain,' grinned Noah ruefully. 'The Macgregor brothers had the beating of us, but Iain said it was age before beauty!'

'Sounds like something Uncle Iain *would* say!' she laughed, returning her attention to the length of silk on the table. 'Simon's taking me to opening night at the Castlebridge Playhouse — I'm wondering whether to make a new dress for the occasion.'

'While we were playing tonight, we were talking about the contraband being brought ashore up-coast,' began Noah awkwardly, watching her smoothing her fingertips across the sheer silk. 'Amaryllis, I know Simon Baldwin told you he bought your presents from a haberdasher's in Liverpool.

'But have you ever wondered how he *really* came by that silk and lace?'

★　★　★

Amaryllis did not spend a restful night.

She'd been angry and shocked at Noah's accusation, and the old childhood pals had had their first ever falling-out.

Amaryllis believed in Simon utterly, and was certain he would *never* have anything to do with contraband. Yet, inexplicably, the notion still nagged at the edges of her mind, allowing her no peace.

Hurrying through her early chores at The Bell, Amaryllis asked her mother if she might be spared for a couple of hours so she could go into St. Agnes. Simon was travelling to York this morning, and would be away several days. Amaryllis desperately needed to see him and as she sped into town, willed she would get there before he left.

* * *

A housemaid showed Amaryllis into a well-appointed reception room at the side of the Baldwin family home, where Simon was occupied, hurriedly making ready for his trip to York.

Despite his kiss of welcome, Amaryllis could not help but feel Simon was less than pleased — perhaps even slightly annoyed — at her being there.

'What's that?' he frowned, indicating the brown paper-wrapped parcel in her arms.

'The presents you gave me for Christmas.' She gazed anxiously up at him. 'Simon, I know you're busy, but I *must* speak — '

'Sorry, Am — whatever it is must wait!' he returned, assiduously resuming his preparations. 'I have an extremely important meeting in Castlebridge, and directly afterwards must board the York coach on company business — '

'This *can't* wait!' she blurted, the

carefully-rehearsed words forgotten in her urgency for Simon's reassurance. 'My presents *aren't* contraband, are they?'

Amaryllis caught her breath, apprehensively searching Simon's face for fear he'd be wounded or disappointed that she could doubt his integrity — but to her horror, Simon laughed out loud, not even pausing with his packing.

'Of course they are! How else but by way of free-traders would one acquire luxury goods in these times of exorbitantly high duties?'

'You got my Christmas presents from *smugglers*?' she cried in disbelief.

'Don't be naïve, Am. Obviously, I don't know the who, where or when — nor do I wish to — but I *do* have a friend who has a friend who knows one or two useful contacts . . . It's the way of the world!'

'It's against the *law*, Simon!' she retorted unsteadily, holding the parcel of gifts out to him. 'I can't accept these now!'

'Judges, parsons, school-teachers; the finest families and the most reputable merchants in the land purchase contraband,' he argued impatiently, firmly pushing the parcel back into her arms. 'It's mere common sense — not to mention sound business — never to pay more for goods than is necessary!'

'You lied to me! Can't you see this changes *everything* between us?' she mumbled brokenly, choking back a sob and spinning away from him before Simon could see her tears. 'It — it's best we don't see one another again — '

'Are you telling me you no longer love me?'

With a single stride Simon reached out, lightly catching her shoulders and arresting Amaryllis's flight through the open doorway.

'All I did was buy a present because I wanted to make you happy.' Simon slowly took a step closer; his hands soothing and caressing Amaryllis's shoulders as he stood behind her, his lips close against her ear when he whispered, 'Was that so very wrong of me?'

Penelope had bided her time and chosen carefully an opportunity to show Adam her preparatory floral sketches and designs for the *Dorothy* tea-set, explaining how their father's plans for Whitlock's to produce the fine, hand-painted line had been set aside upon his falling ill last year.

She and Adam hadn't had much to say to one another of late. He'd been furious after discovering Penelope had defied him and gone ahead with the family tradition of giving Goode's Day buns and Christmas boxes to the pot-workers, and left her in no doubt he deeply resented and would not tolerate her interference in the pottery's affairs.

Thus, Penelope had been astounded and greatly heartened when Adam immediately approved the *Dorothy* and gave his permission to manufacture the line. That this special tea-set would be dedicated to their mother — and Adam was surely aware how much it meant to their father — had perhaps made the difference to his attitude?

Watching her young brother riding from the Grange with his bailiff, Gerrard, at his right hand, Penelope hoped she and Adam might now be able to set aside their recent differences and work harmoniously together at their family's pottery.

★   ★   ★

The tall, slender-necked chimneys of Whitlock's enormous brick-built, bottle-shaped kilns rose up into the grey, smoke-streaked sky above Akenside, and were a landmark for miles around the cramped, noisy industrial town.

Manoeuvring narrow, winding streets congested with waggons, carts, drays, drovers and pack-horses, Penelope passed Lathom's Dyeworks. It was one of the largest factories in Akenside but curiously, its yards were empty and there was neither sound nor any sign of activity from the huge building itself.

She rode on through the town and into the gates of Whitlock's, the elderly cocky watchman hurrying from his hut to meet her.

'Top o' the mornin' to you, Miss Penny!'

'And the rest of the day to yourself, Mr Doyle!' she laughed, returning the greeting they'd exchanged since Penelope was a little girl coming here with her father. 'I've just passed Lathom's, and it looks deserted!'

'It is,' he answered with a sniff. 'They've gone. Packed up.'

'Lathom's have closed down?' she echoed incredulously. 'Lathom's was here long before even Father set up in Akenside!'

'Three generations of 'em,' nodded Mr Doyle sagely. 'It's grandsons run the works now. Talk is, they sold out to Frazer's and made a fortune on the deal.'

'Frazer's? They have dyeworks across county in Gorsey, don't they?'

'Aye, but they've got no canal over

their way, so they're moving their works lock, stock and barrel down here because of the Cut,' he declared. 'Lathom's may be the first to sell up but mark my words, they'll not be the last to take the money and run.

'Times in Akenside are changing, Miss Penny — changing right before our eyes!'

★   ★   ★

Having rubbed down and rugged Sorrel, Penelope gave the grey mare fresh hay and water before stabling her and walking around past the bottle-kilns and across the pottery's yard to the master's house.

She first went up into the hand-painters' room. It was south-facing with the largest windows, so gave the best light for the women decorating Whitlock's finest ware. Penelope gave them the good news about the *Dorothy* and, spreading her sketches across one of the benches, asked the painters their opinion as to which pattern would work best upon this very special tea-set. They discussed the merits of each design at considerable length before Penelope went downstairs to her father's old office. After almost a whole year's disuse, it was in a sorry state.

Penelope had raked out the grate and lit a fire, and was tackling the room's accumulated dust and grime, when the pottery's overlooker stuck his head around the open door.

'Grand news about the *Dorothy*, Miss Penny — and better yet that you're back with us!'

'I'm here only to work on the tea-set, Albert. In no other capacity,' she stressed. Carefully, she added, 'But . . . it is a *beginning*, isn't it?'

'It is that! By, you've a right job in here,' he remarked, taking in the long-neglected office. 'I'll send over a couple of lasses to clean it out for you.'

'Thanks, Albert,' she replied with a small smile, 'but I want to do this myself.'

'Aye, I'll leave you to it,' he nodded, understanding. 'If you need owt, you know where to find me!'

Although it would take more than one session's sweeping, scrubbing and dusting to restore Elias's office to its customary orderliness, Penelope was satisfied with her efforts by the time she trimmed the wick and lit the lamp in the late afternoon.

Removing her apron and rolling down her sleeves, she settled behind her father's desk, adjusting the ink wells and pen tray to better suit her reach, and took up the *Dorothy* sketches once more. She was deliberating upon handle shapes when the door of her office swung open and Adam strode within.

'I see you haven't wasted any time getting your feet under the master's desk!' he announced heartily. 'My sincere wishes for success with your tea-set, Pen!'

The sudden interruption startled her, and Penelope glanced up sharply from her work. Adam was standing over her, grinning broadly. She met his gaze and witnessed not warmth and welcome, but something dangerously akin to *warning* in her young brother's shrewd eyes.

'Whitlock's is mine now,' he murmured softly. 'You'll do well to remember that!'

★ ★ ★

Amaryllis was always first up at The Bell.

She lit the shaded candle, washed and dressed without Betsy and Flossie stirring and went noiselessly down the stairs. After raking out the cold ashes and lighting the inn-house's fires, she set fresh water to boil for tea and the family's breakfast porridge to cook before returning upstairs to waken Dorcas.

Dorcas never liked getting up in the morning, however when Amaryllis had twice tapped upon her door without hearing any response from within, she went inside and immediately saw the room was empty.

Lighting the candle, she saw although the patchwork quilt was rumpled, the bed clearly had not been slept in. The candle-flame's soft, flickering light fell upon the looking-glass on Dorcas's little dressing-table — and Amaryllis spotted the note wedged into its corner.

Without hesitation, she flew past her parents' room and downstairs, racing through the inn-house and into the inn itself, up the turned staircase and along to Kit's rooms at the end of the landing.

'Dorcas has run off!' she whispered the instant Kit's door opened.

★   ★   ★

Kit lost no time joining Amaryllis in the stables, where she was hastily saddling Patch in readiness for Kit to give chase to the eloping lovers.

'I'm riding directly to Haddonsell — oh, no! I don't believe Whitlock will have taken Dorcas to the Grange,' he explained quickly, seeing the question spring to his sister's anxious eyes, 'but I intend asking Penny to accompany me on the journey. When we catch up with the couple, another woman's presence will be sorely needed.'

'Yes, I can see that,' agreed Amaryllis, going on uneasily, 'in the note, Dorcas says they're getting married . . . but what if Adam — '

'Try not to worry, Amaryllis,' murmured Kit, taking Patch's reins from her cold hands. 'Get on with the day as usual, and do all you can to reassure your parents.

'I promise you — No harm will come to Dorcas!'

*   *   *

'It happens I *do* know something of Gretna Green,' remarked Penelope thoughtfully. Still clad in nightclothes, she was reading Dorcas's note for a second time.

She and Kit were in her sitting-room at the Grange, and Penelope's maid had already gone out to the stables to ascertain whether Adam had taken horses or was driving the Whitlock carriage.

'When we were young, my friend Lydia had a fancy about eloping and told me a great deal about marriage at Gretna Green,' went on Penelope, returning the note to Kit. 'Couples arriving in the village can be married immediately by the blacksmith at his forge. It's a handfasting ceremony and, according to Lydia, the marriage is declared when the blacksmith strikes his hammer on the anvil.'

'I'm impressed!' Kit raised an eyebrow. 'Miss Unsworth is a fount of information!'

'You don't know the half of it!' She returned his smile wryly. 'It's a lengthy journey, Kit. Even travelling in haste, Dorcas and Adam will need to overnight somewhere at least once before crossing the border into Scotland — '

'Miss! I knocked the groom up and he says Mr Adam's horse and one other have gone,' Margaret darted into the sitting-room, a coat thrown over her nightgown and her hair still in curl papers. 'I told him to get Sorrel ready as quick as he can!

'I'll go up to pack your valise and set out your travelling clothes.' The maid hovered in the doorway, glancing back to Penelope. 'Miss . . . When the master and missus wake up, what'll I tell them?'

'Tell them the truth. That Adam and Miss Macgregor have eloped to Gretna Green and Kit and I are joining them to bear witness at their marriage,' replied Penelope simply. 'Thanks for your help, Margaret — I'm sorry you've had a disturbed night.'

'That's all right, miss!' Bobbing her head, the maid scurried out, leaving Penelope and Kit alone.

'I'll hurry and dress — ' She paused, kissing him. ' — and we'll be on our way to Scotland!'

'It'll be a grand match!' Ethel was saying, her face red and perspiring from the exertion of using both hands and all her strength turning the heavy handle of the mangle. 'Aye, it *was* a bit of a shock at breakfast when you told your pa and me the news, but now I've had a few hours to get used to it, I'm right happy for Dorcas!'

Daylight came late on these winter mornings, and she and Amaryllis were in the inn's wash-house, their work lit by the dull gleam of thick, stubby candles standing in glass jars to magnify their brightness.

'Oh, I can't deny I would've loved to see our Dorcas walk down the aisle to wed Adam Whitlock right here in our own church,' finished Ethel wistfully, putting her back into the mangling. 'But I'm sure they've eloped because Dorcas knew fine well your pa wouldn't consent to her marrying Mr Adam. And seeing as she won't come of age till the back-end of the year . . . Well, happen this way is for the best.'

'It's time we swapped over, Ma,' said Amaryllis. She'd been folding wet laundry and feeding it between the great rollers; now she stepped aside and took her mother's place at the handle. 'I wonder where Dorcas is.'

'I have *heard* of Gretna Green,' remarked Ethel, hefting a bed-sheet from the heap of dripping laundry. 'Years ago, I read in the newspaper about the daughter of some lord or other who eloped with the family's butler to Gretna Green. But her father's men caught up with the couple before they got wed and took her home again.'

'Do you suppose Kit and Miss Whitlock have caught up with Dorcas yet?'

'I don't know. It's a long way — right up into Scotland — but they'll catch up sooner or later,' she replied confidently. 'And I'm glad Kit and Miss Whitlock went after them. It'll look better this way.

'Not that I doubt young Mr Adam, you understand. He's a gentleman, and he'll do right by Dorcas,' went on Ethel practically. 'But having Kit and Miss Whitlock travelling with the couple to their wedding makes it more . . . *proper*. Chaperones, sort of. So there's no cause for gossip. You know how folk round here like tittle-tattling about other folks' business!'

Stooping to haul another bundle of wet washing, she suddenly paused. Standing up straight, and drawing a deep, contented breath.

'Mrs Adam Whitlock of Haddonsell Grange,' murmured Ethel, her eyes shining with love and pride. 'Our Dorcas has turned her last mangle, Am!'

Several hours after Kit and Penelope started upon the long road north, they reached the commodious King's Head post inn. While Penelope tended and watered their horses, Kit stepped inside to enquire after the eloping lovers.

'The landlord says Dorcas and Adam

were here very early this morning,' he related, joining Penelope at the trough. 'Apparently, Adam gave instructions for the two horses they'd been riding to be taken back to Haddonsell Grange, and made arrangements to hire a coach and driver for the rest of their journey.

'Dorcas asked the landlord's wife about places of interest along the route, and quality shops where items of fashion might be purchased,' Kit went on, swinging up into Patch's saddle. 'The young lady and gentleman then took a hearty and leisurely breakfast before going on their way in the hired coach.'

'I'd assumed eloping couples travelled at breakneck speed to reach Gretna Green,' mused Penelope, following Kit from the post inn's yard and out onto the north road. 'Dorcas and Adam appear to be taking their time, as though on an excursion, stopping here and there to see the sights and do some shopping.'

'They certainly aren't in any hurry to

be married, are they?' frowned Kit, adding, 'then again, the slower their progress, the sooner we'll catch up with them.'

It was late that same evening when Kit and Penelope rode up a broad, elm-lined drive and around an ornamental lake to the Tarleton Hall Hotel, where they found Dorcas and Adam Whitlock enjoying an intimate dinner.

* * *

'As I live and breathe! If it isn't my older sister and her engineer friend,' exclaimed Adam genially, raising his glass in salutation when Kit and Penelope were shown into the private dining-room. 'I regret you're too late for dinner, but you'll join us for brandy, coffee, liqueurs, perhaps?'

'I think not,' replied Kit quietly, his concern focussed upon Dorcas. 'Are you quite well, Dorcas?'

'How *dare* you follow me!' she hissed, glowering across the exquisitely-dressed dining table at him, her green eyes bright with anger and indignation. 'I'm not going back home with you! I'm staying with Adam!'

'What brings you and my dear sister here, Chesterton?' enquired Adam complacently, taking Dorcas's hand and raising it to his lips. 'The lady is at my side of her own choosing. You really have no business interfering.'

'You're mistaken, Whitlock,' responded Kit, lowering his voice. 'I'm Dorcas's only brother, and have responsibility for her wellbeing.

'Why don't we leave the ladies to their coffee,' he concluded. 'While you and I repair to the gentlemen's smoking-room and discuss your precise intentions?'

⋆ ⋆ ⋆

Ethel and Amaryllis were hanging new curtains in the back parlour of the inn-house when Betsy and Flossie careered in from the yard.

'It's from *Dorcas*!' cried Betsy, waving the letter wildly. 'It's come with the south-bound mail coach!'

Setting aside her end of the curtains, Ethel took the letter. She held it with both hands and gazed at Dorcas's familiar writing. What with Kit and Miss Whitlock accompanying the couple to Gretna Green, she was certain everything *would've* turned out right . . . Yet Ethel still felt apprehensive about opening the letter, lest . . . But no! Such notions were sheer foolishness. Hurriedly breaking the seal, Ethel unfolded the page and swiftly scanned its lines.

'Dorcas is wed!' she beamed, looking up to Amaryllis and Betsy. 'And see — she's signed her letter *Mrs Adam Whitlock!*'

Passing the page to her daughters so they might read it for themselves, Ethel went on to relate its contents in detail.

'She says they were married at the blacksmith's forge, and Mr Adam gave her a beautiful ring and a bejewelled bracelet! Directly after the ceremony, they left Kit and Miss Whitlock and set off on their wedding trip!

'Dorcas wrote this letter on the way to Harrogate, where they're to visit friends of Adam's from his India days. Then they're going all the way down to London for the theatres and shops, and when Dorcas told Adam she'd heard Bath was an exceedingly cultivated and fashionable place and had always dreamed of going there, he said then go there they must!

'They're to stay in Bath a while before coming home, then they'll live at Haddonsell Grange before establishing their own household in Castlebridge — oh!' Ethel broke off abruptly, her thoughts racing nineteen-to-the-dozen. 'They'll not have had a wedding cake, nor anything like!

'Girls, we need to bake them a proper Lancashire marriage cake. We'll do that straight away so the cake will have time to mellow nicely before Dorcas and her husband get back from their wedding trip!'

Ethel quickly made a list of ingredients and, since Amaryllis and Noah Pendleton had already arranged to drive into St. Agnes for The Bell's weekly errands, Ethel seized the opportunity to accompany them in the mill's heavy cart.

Upon reaching the prosperous little market town, the three went their separate ways. Ethel made a beeline for Pickersgill's. It was a fine grocery with well-stocked shelves and was always busy. She wasn't in the least surprised to find a cluster of womenfolk in the shop and knew all of them. Nodding politely to her friends and neighbours, Ethel didn't notice their conversation falling silent as she entered. Nor their sly nudges and inquisitive glances when she took her place in the queue.

''Afternoon, Mrs Macgregor.' Annie Pickersgill cleared her throat. 'What can I get you?'

'Oh, I can't jump my turn!' protested Ethel cheerfully, smiling around at the gathered ladies. 'Besides, I've a very long list today!'

'You go on ahead of us, Ethel,' urged Peggy Travis, the churchwarden's wife. 'We're not in any hurry.'

'Shopping for something special, are you?' queried a thin woman in a poke bonnet, craning her neck to glimpse Ethel's lengthy list.

'My daughter Dorcas and Mr Adam Whitlock — of Haddonsell Grange, you know? — are married!' Bursting with pride, Ethel could not help but tell everybody all about it. 'I'm baking a proper Lancashire marriage cake, to celebrate the happy couple's homecoming when they get back from their wedding trip. They're going to Bath; after they've been to Harrogate and London, of course.'

'Mercy me, Ethel — now you have *two* new members of your family,' remarked the lady in the poke bonnet maliciously. 'Dorcas's husband — and Sandy's baseborn son from Jamaica!'

7

Shocked and humiliated, Ethel stood stock-still.

Passing the tip of her tongue across dry lips, she was scarce able to draw breath. Snatching up her shopping list from the counter, Ethel turned on her heel and marched from the grocery, closing its door quietly behind her.

Once outside in the keen winter's air, Ethel's trembling hand flew to her mouth, her composure crumbling as she scurried blindly along the market town's busy high street.

'*Ma!*' Emerging from Great Aunt Macgregor's shop with an armful of Betsy's lesson-books, Amaryllis caught sight of her mother and ran to her side. 'Whatever's wrong?'

'They all *know*,' mumbled Ethel, casting an anguished glance at Amaryllis.

'The whole of St. Agnes is tittle-tattling about us!'

* ★ ★ ★

'I'll fetch Noah to drive you home,' Amaryllis was saying, ushering Ethel toward the heavy mill-cart and gently taking the shopping list clutched within her mother's cold hands. 'I'll see to the shopping, and once we're home we'll bake Dorcas's marriage cake.

'Wait here, Ma — I shan't be long!'

She found Noah Pendleton in the chandler's, and hurriedly explained as they sped back across town. 'So will you take Ma home, please?' Amaryllis finished, turning away as they approached the cart.

'Of course — but where are *you* going?' he asked in surprise. 'Aren't you coming with us?'

Amaryllis shook her head, her face set. 'I'll call at the grocer's to get these ingredients; then there's somebody I must see here in town.'

'Surely — '

'This can't wait, Noah,' she replied, silencing his protest. 'Take care of Ma. She's upset. I'll make my own way home.'

★   ★   ★

Simon Baldwin was smoking a cigar and perusing the newspaper when the parlour-maid showed Amaryllis in.

'What an unexpected pleasure!' he beamed, rising to greet her with hands outstretched. 'To what do I owe this — '

'When I told you Kit was my brother, you gave your word it would go no further,' snapped Amaryllis, stepping clear of his embrace. 'Yet it seems all St. Agnes knows — and only *you* can be responsible, Simon!'

'Oh, Am — *mea culpa*! I had no idea people were gossiping,' he groaned, slapping his forehead with the heel of his hand. 'I humbly apologise, and beg your forgiveness!

'I swear, I never meant to break my promise. I was playing cards here in town with some of the chaps. We were having a rare old night, putting the world to rights, drinking double-Hollands, talking as fellows will . . . ' Simon appeared genuinely abashed and, drawing closer, touched Amaryllis's hand with his fingertips.

For the first time, Amaryllis did not respond to Simon's touch. 'You haven't any notion of the hurt and distress you've caused, have you?'

'I'm truly sorry; but after all, the truth was bound to come out sooner or later, wasn't it?' he murmured persuasively. 'You can't keep something like *that* quiet forever!'

Without another word, Simon moved nearer.

'I — I never want to see you again.' Amaryllis stood fast before the man she'd believed herself in love with, meeting his gaze steadily. 'All is over between us, Simon.'

The handfasting ceremony bound

Adam Whitlock and Dorcas Macgregor as man and wife immediately, and their marriage was declared across the blacksmith's anvil. The couple quit Gretna Green, boarding their coach and taking the road for the ancient spa town of Harrogate.

In contrast, Kit and Penelope weren't in any hurry to resume travelling. They chose to put up at the village inn, crossing the Scottish border on the morrow and setting out upon the long road south.

'I'm declining the Birmingham investors' commission,' Kit remarked, while he and Penelope rode unhurried down toward the lakes' country. It'd started snowing earlier, and they'd already decided to break their journey and rest the horses at the Tarleton Hall Hotel. 'I'll write with my decision directly we're home.'

'Are you certain, Kit? Constructing a shorter route between Birmingham and the River Severn is a worthwhile enterprise,' she commented. 'Are you refusing this commission because of your commitment to the Akenside Cut?'

'The investors are aware it will be some time before I'd be free to move on from the Cut,' he responded, looking across to Penelope riding at his side. Snowfall was light now, dusting her hair and bonnet. A single snowflake clung to Penelope's eyelashes, and Kit watched her brushing it away with a gloved hand.

'The truth is, I don't want to be free and I don't want to move on,' he murmured, gazing into blue eyes that seemed even bluer in the uncanny brightness of this snowy morning. 'I want to stay in Lancashire. With you.

'Will you marry me, Penny?'

*   *   *

Snow continued falling for much of the day, and when they finally approached Tarleton Hall, it was to discover a most lively ice party in full swing on the frozen lake. Flaring torches and gaily-coloured lanterns illuminated its banks; musicians clustered around a brazier while playing merry reels and jigs; and relays of hotel staff muffled against the cold slithered back and forth, keeping Tarleton Hall's wealthy guests liberally supplied with hot roasted chestnuts, negus and spiced ales.

'What *will* you do after Akenside?' ventured Penelope practically, while they were putting on borrowed skates. 'You're an engineer, Kit. You must surely go wherever your work takes you?'

'I design and build things,' he shrugged, smiling. 'I'll find something to design and build in Lancashire.'

'Yes,' Penelope persisted. 'But — '

'Have you heard of James Brindley? Or John Smeaton?' interrupted Kit blithely. 'When I was a boy at boarding school, I read everything I could about their work and that of other men like them. Brindley built the Bridgwater, and his aqueduct carrying the canal over the River Irwell was hailed an engineering wonder.

'Smeaton was another canal-builder, but he was also responsible for the design and construction of bridges, harbours and lighthouses. There'll be plenty of engineering challenges for me close to home,' he reassured, lacing up her skates. 'Perhaps I'll follow Smeaton's example and build a lighthouse on our very doorstep — how would that be?'

They both smiled now, Kit drawing Penelope to her feet so they might take to the ice.

'I know you were joking — about the lighthouse — but the waters along our stretch of coastline *are* known to be treacherous, Kit,' she began thoughtfully. 'Many a vessel comes to grief making its way to or from Liverpool. Landmarks are well and good, but a proper lighthouse would be a godsend.'

'That's it, then!' He laughed softly, and hand-in-hand they skimmed across the frozen lake to the lively rhythms of a fiddler's waltz. 'Soon as the Cut is navigable, I'll build a lighthouse at Macgregor's Cove!'

★　★　★

After spending those very special days alone with Penelope, parting from her was even more of a wrench than usual.

Reluctantly leaving her at Haddonsell Grange, Kit rode out to Macgregor's Cove. There hadn't been any snow here, but the night was bitterly cold with barely a sliver of pale moon; the receding tide lay flat and shrouded in shifting sea mist.

The Bell's yard was empty as Kit led Patch into the warmth of the stables. He rubbed down and rugged the weary mare, examining her hoofs and shoes before leaving her to feed and settle for the night.

He went up into the inn. Apart from three elderly regulars who collected in their corner drinking ale day in, day

out, eating hotpot and playing bonesticks, everywhere was still and Sandy
was alone.

He was seated comfortably before the
fire with a tot of rum, contemplating
the glowing logs and enjoying a pipe.

'It's good to see you're keeping busy!'
declared Kit, taking off his hat and
coat.

'You should've been here an hour
since,' muttered Sandy grimly. 'The
Leeds coach was late so the Chester
arrived right on its tail, Noah brought
in the Manx packet, then two carriages
showed up with a family of seven
wanting room and board for three
nights — I've only just got shut of the
lot of 'em.' He glanced sidelong at his
son, adding with a long-suffering sigh, 'I
suppose I'd better get up and fetch you
summat to drink, seeing as how you've
come all the way from Scotland . . . '

'Stay where you are. I'll help myself.'
Kit indicated the three elderly men in
the corner. 'Shall I refill their jug of
ale?'

'Might as well. Save them having to stir and ask for it.'

With that done, Kit brought his glass over to the fireside. 'What's been happening here?'

'Baking. Ethel and the girls have made Dorcas's marriage cake. Huge, it is. Big as a quern. We got another letter from her today,' he went on, sipping his rum. 'They're in Harrogate. Staying with friends of his. She says she's drunk the waters. Bought some hats, and she's having a promenade frock made — whatever that is. She's having a high old time.'

Kit nodded, enquiring after a moment, 'What do you make of Adam Whitlock?'

'I like him fine well,' Sandy replied at once. 'You never see him lording it over ordinary folk, like many of his sort do. Adam's a good man — but he's not our class!

'Adam Whitlock's gentry, and she's daughter of a country innkeeper. I don't want her to get hurt, Kit — or be ashamed of who she is and where she comes from.' Sandy Macgregor swirled the dregs of the Jamaican dark rum around his glass. 'I hope our Dorcas never has cause to regret marrying above herself!'

* * *

Penelope slipped effortlessly back into the daily routine of managing Whitlock's.

She worked from the front downstairs room of the master's house, rarely venturing up to the top floor and the office her brother used. Although Penelope had admitted it only to Kit, she was glad Adam was taking a lengthy wedding trip and in no haste to return to the pottery.

Winter days were lengthening toward spring, and she and Kit frequently rode into Akenside together. Although recent heavy rains and some flooding had slowed the Cut's construction, after a spell of dry days Penelope seized the opportunity to accompany Kit to the workings with her sketchbook.

'Father looks forward to seeing everything taking shape,' she was saying, sketching with a few skilful strokes the channel where barges and boats would moor up for loading and discharging cargo. 'Despite delays, the wharf's coming along in leaps and bounds, isn't it?'

'It'll be the first section of the Cut to be finished,' nodded Kit, who was also Surveyor of Works. 'Are you coming over to The Bell for supper this evening?'

Penelope shook her head, putting away her pencils and sketchbook and crossing to where she'd tethered Sorrel. 'I promised Mother I'd help make ready for Adam and Dorcas's home-coming.'

★ ★ ★

'What do you think of these rooms for them, Penny?' asked Dorothy. They were standing in a beautifully-proportioned room on Haddonsell Grange's second floor; its windows overlooked the gardens, and other rooms opened off to either side. 'There's very good light, if Dorcas likes to sew or draw. And I'm having the pianoforte brought up, because Mrs Macgregor mentioned Dorcas enjoys playing.'

'I'm sure Dorcas will be delighted!' reassured Penelope warmly, slipping her arm through Dorothy's.

'I want her to feel at home while she's here, Penny. Comfortable, you know? Not like she's a guest in somebody else's house,' explained Dorothy earnestly. 'It's important for a new wife to know she has her *own* place — somewhere she can close the door and call her own.'

★   ★   ★

Penelope smuggled the small wooden crate she'd brought home from the pottery into her father's room.

233

'Is that what I think it is?' Elias's drawn face lit up.

Nodding, Penelope carefully prised open the lid. Moving layers of straw and wadding, she revealed a cup, saucer and side plate, together with the sugar bowl, milk jug and teapot from the *Dorothy* hand-painted floral tea-set.

'It's *beautiful*!' mumbled Elias, overcome. He'd wanted to throw this set himself, dedicating it to his beloved wife — but illness put paid to that. 'You and everyone at the pot-works have done a fine job, Penny. A *fine* job!'

'We know how much the *Dorothy* means to you, Father,' she responded, an unexpected lump coming to her throat. 'You'd wanted to surprise Mother with it on her birthday last year . . . Making this tea-set meant a lot to us all!'

It was absolutely true. These past weeks, during her brother's absence, Penelope sensed the mood around the pottery shifting. It was difficult to pin down, but folk were cheerful again.

234

Going about their work with a will, like old times. The times before Adam came from India to take over the family firm.

Penelope hadn't breathed a word of the disturbing conversation she'd had with Albert Thwaite on Christmas Eve, when the overseer had complained about Adam's negligent management of Whitlock's — and she was determined Elias should never hear of it.

' . . . The line can go into production as soon as it fits with whatever else we've on the books,' Elias was saying, his mind ticking over as sharply as ever when it came to the pottery. 'Quality work like this'll tie up the best painters and gilders. Take on extra hands if you need them, Penny. Put a bit extra in everybody's wages this week, too — they've earned it. Be sure and tell them thank you from me.

'Will you hide the full set where your mother can't find it?' he finished, a tad breathlessly, watching Penelope packing the pieces back into the crate. 'We'll surprise Dotty with it on her birthday *this* year — better late than never, eh?'

'I'll put it on top of my book-shelves,' beamed Penelope. It did her heart good seeing her father happy and full of life again. 'Mother isn't tall enough to see up there!'

'She's been busier than my bees getting ready for Adam bringing Dorcas home,' remarked Elias. 'Even though they'll not be here two blinks before they move to Castlebridge — into *Rishton Place*, no less!

'I'm right proud of Adam,' continued Elias meditatively, easing more comfortably into the huge winged chair alongside the window. 'I sent the lad off to India with next to nowt in his pockets, but he worked hard and made good. Came back a man of means, with fortune enough to take a fine house in Rishton Place for him and his new wife.

'It wasn't fair, y'know. Expecting Adam to give up everything in India to come home and take over here,' he admitted, frowning. 'I couldn't have blamed him if he resented it.

'But he's never complained! He's just knuckled down and got on with it. That's not easy for an ambitious young man with his whole life in front of him, Penny.

'Not easy at all!'

* * *

'Now the excitement is over and, for the time being at least, Dorcas and her new husband are settled at Haddonsell Grange,' Mathilda Macgregor was telling Amaryllis while they planted shallot bulbs in the sunny, well-drained soil of The Bell's kitchen garden, 'I've decided to pay our Manx cousins a long overdue visit — and I suggest you and Betsy accompany me.

'I've spoken to Noah,' she concluded. 'Our passage is arranged aboard the packet's next sailing.'

Amaryllis stared at her in astonishment. 'Betsy and I can't possibly go away — not *now!*'

'These past months haven't been the

easiest for your parents,' countered Mathilda firmly. 'Nonetheless, they've kept the family — and the inn — running like clockwork. I doubt they've had any time together to think and take stock.'

'But now Dorcas has gone,' protested Amaryllis earnestly, 'however will Ma and Pa manage if Betsy and I aren't here?'

Mathilda Macgregor almost smiled.

'Child, your mother and father ran The Bell perfectly competently long before you and your sisters arrived in this world,' she replied drily. 'I daresay they'll muddle along without you for a wee while!'

★   ★   ★

On the morning the girls were sailing to the Isle of Man, Ethel came from the inn-house with a baking basket over her arm, and crossed the yard to the stable where Kit was saddling Patch.

'I've made a batch of goosnargh for Am and Betsy's journey. Thought you might like to take some to work,' she began, offering the muslin-wrapped parcel. 'It's a pity you can't go with the girls and meet your Manx cousins.'

Kit thanked her for the shortbread rounds, adding. 'Yes, I'd like to have gone. I can't be away from the Cut just now, though. We're due to start puddling the wharf.'

'You must go next time, then. Perhaps take Miss Whitlock with you?' Ethel met his eyes a shade awkwardly, before rushing on. 'Kit . . . I never did thank you for what you — and Miss Whitlock — did for our Dorcas. You were a true brother, and I'll not forget it.

'Well.' With a quick smile and bob of her head, she hurried away. 'I'd best make sure the girls are packing what's needed.'

★   ★   ★

She and Sandy stood on the quayside beyond The Bell, waving off the Manx packet.

'You're wearing your new gansey,' remarked Ethel. She'd been knitting it in her kitchen the day Sandy came indoors and told her about Marietta. 'I've not seen it since I gave it to you on Christmas.'

'It — er — it didn't seem right putting it on,' he mumbled, fidgeting with the thick ribbing on the sleeve. 'It's a grand gansey. Best I've ever seen.'

'Aunt Mathilda found the pattern for me. She says it's been in your family for generations. Came down from Scotland with the Macgregors.'

They fell silent, watching the packet sailing into open sea.

'I'm sorry I never told you about Marietta!' blurted Sandy, struggling to explain and stumbling over his words. 'When I went to Jobert Town and heard they were both dead, I come home. But I didn't tell anybody what'd happened. Not even Dad or Iain. I — I just *couldn't*!

'Nobody ever knew. Nobody.' He shook his head, avoiding her searching gaze. 'Years went by, and when you and me started walking out . . . Well, I suppose it was just easier not looking back.'

'I can understand how that could be,' she acknowledged soberly. 'And we have been blessed with a good life. Here with our girls.'

'I don't want to lose you,' he muttered awkwardly. 'Are we alright, Ethel — thee and me?'

'Aye, we're alright, Sandy Macgregor.' She nodded, her stern features softening into a small smile. 'Always were, and I daresay always will be.'

With the Manx packet fading from sight on the swell of the tide, they turned from the quayside and started up toward the inn-house.

★   ★   ★

'Penny suggested it some while ago, and since then I've given the notion considerable thought.' Kit paused, waiting while Elias Whitlock made his

241

move on the chessboard between them. 'I canvassed Sandy and Iain's opinions, and they believe a permanent light — possibly a *pair* of lights, higher and lower — would greatly assist safer navigation through the approaches and on into Liverpool.'

'They're the men who'll know,' agreed Elias. 'Born and bred in the cove from a family of boat-builders, and Sandy himself a seaman. Trinity House'd be in charge of construction, I suppose?'

'Not necessarily. Many lighthouses are built by private entrepreneurs,' commented Kit, pondering the chess-board. 'I've already completed some preliminary drawings, and as soon as work on the Cut allows, I'll begin a thorough survey.'

'You intend staying in these parts, then?'

'There's no doubt about that, Elias!' He raised his face, smiling broadly. 'Lighthouse or no lighthouse — *this* is where I'm finally putting down roots!'

'Happen you and Penny'll have plans of your own for after you're wed,' began the older man after a moment, meeting Kit's eyes. 'But if the pair of you ever want to make Haddonsell Grange your home, there's nowt'd make me and Dotty happier!'

* * *

' . . . as usual, your ma said to tell you all's well,' related Noah Pendleton.

While Amaryllis was visiting her Manx cousins, Noah had taken up to going to the Macgregor's croft whenever he sailed across to the island, calling upon her with messages from home.

'They've taken on a girl. Widow Watkins recommended her, and she's doing grand. She's daughter of one of Widow Watkins's friends.'

'That *is* good news!' exclaimed Amaryllis. After Dorcas married, The Bell had needed another pair of hands. 'I'm glad she's settling in — there's a lot to learn!'

The pair strolled on, Noah offering a steadying hand as they scrambled over slippery, mossy stones and down into the glen. It was a fine, early summer's day and they'd been up to the ancient kirk where the first Macgregors to settle on Man had once worshipped.

'Is there a chance you and Simon Baldwin will make up?' he queried unexpectedly.

'Certainly not,' replied Amaryllis emphatically, going on slowly, 'you were right about him. I'm terribly sorry for the things I said to you, Noah — and for our falling out.'

'We had words right enough,' he agreed with a small smile. 'But we never really fell out, Amaryllis! You and me, we've been . . . *pals* . . . far too long for that to ever happen.'

Holding onto Noah's hand a little more tightly, Amaryllis cautiously edged along the split oak-bole bridging the swift stream.

'If Betsy and little Cousin Lachlan were with us,' she said, her voice not quite steady, 'they'd tell us to be sure and wish the fairy folk good-morning while we're crossing the burn!'

'*Moghrey mie*, then!' laughed Noah, slipping a protective arm about her as they traversed the deep, clear water.

★ ★ ★

Amaryllis and Noah hadn't long returned to the Macgregors' croft when Flossie's joyous barking drew them to the farmhouse's open door. Betsy, Lachlan and Flossie were hurtling up the path, while Great Aunt Mathilda and Morag Macgregor followed at a more dignified gait.

'We've been to the clog-maker and I have my clogs!' cried Betsy, proudly showing off her new footwear. 'They're *exactly* like Lachlan's!'

'They're beauties,' admired Amaryllis, glancing at Morag as they went indoors. 'I may ask Mr Watterson to make pairs for Ma and me, too!'

'You'll not go wrong with Watterson's

clogs,' opined Morag Macgregor. 'I'd be lost about the croft without mine.'

'While we were in the village collecting my clogs,' went on Betsy, fetching a dish of fresh water for Flossie, 'we saw those men who chased us from the ruins at Christmastide!'

'Killip and Gerrard?' echoed Amaryllis, turning to Noah in consternation. 'Whatever could *they* be doing here?'

'I have spotted Killip here several times — he's a Manx fisherman, so it's only to be expected,' replied Noah thoughtfully. 'But Gerrard? What reason would Adam Whitlock's *bailiff* have for being on the island? And how has he got here? He's never sailed aboard the packet!'

'He — the bigger man — *has* been here before, but I know nothing of him,' put in Morag Macgregor, sensing the tension of their conversation. 'I know plenty about the other one, though! He may call himself Killip when he's on the mainland, but he's a Faragher! One of five brothers, and you want to keep well away from them all. They're a wicked breed.

'Like their father before them, the Faragher brothers make their money smuggling — and far worse besides!'

★ ★ ★

The instant Penelope rode through the gates of Whitlock's, she realised something was terribly wrong.

A knot of grim-faced workers stood in the yard, talking in low voices to the pottery's overseer; others scurried silently about their duties, heads bowed and eyes fixed upon the grimy cobbles.

'What's going on, Mr Doyle?' she asked when the cocky-watchman hurried from his hut to greet her. 'Has there been an accident? Is somebody hurt?'

'It's not that — '

Before the elderly watchman could finish, Albert Thwaite broke from the pot-workers and came to her. 'I need a word, Miss Penny.'

Once within the master's house, she led the way into her front-room office and closed the door. 'Whatever's wrong, Albert?'

'There's talk Whitlock's is selling up to a firm bringing in its own workers,' he returned tersely. 'Is it right t'pot-works is closing down and we'll all be out us jobs?'

*   *   *

The question — the *accusation* — struck Penelope like a blow to the chest.

Far worse was being unable to immediately quash the rumour and set everybody's mind at rest, for this was the first Penelope had heard of a sale.

Her brother had not been into Whitlock's this whole week. Since returning from his wedding trip, Adam was devoting even less of his time and interest to the pottery.

Penelope rarely entered Adam's office on the top floor of the master's house. Now though, she did so, setting about a thorough search.

* * *

The correspondence from Sydney Parker & Sons was burning a hole in Penelope's pocket, but there was no opportunity to confront Adam until after dinner at Haddonsell Grange, when she sought him out in their father's study.

The door was slightly ajar. She could hear her brother speaking with Gerrard, and waited until the bailiff quit the study before entering. Adam was standing over by the sideboard, pouring brandy from one of the heavy crystal decanters. Without a word, Penelope crossed the room and set Parkers' letters down on the walnut sideboard.

'You've stolen those from my office!' exclaimed Adam. Rather than being angry, a grin of amazement creased his handsome face and he raised his glass to Penelope. 'You rise in my estimation, old girl!'

'You intend selling Whitlock's to this cotton manufacturer?'

'Since those letters are evidence, there's little point denying it,' he remarked mildly, taking a seat on the couch. 'Thanks to Father bringing the canal to Akenside, property there — and especially *land* — are as gold-dust. Parkers' made an excellent offer. Only a fool would refuse.'

'Father doesn't know anything about this deal, does he?'

'Not yet. I planned upon waiting until proceedings were rather more advanced.' He shrugged his shoulders in a helpless gesture. 'Ah, but the best laid plans . . . If I don't tell Father at once, I'm sure you will!'

'What were you thinking of, Adam? Or were you thinking at all?' she challenged angrily. 'Our workers' livelihoods are at stake! And have you even considered Father? He built Whitlock's from nothing to pass on to *you!* It's his life's work — '

'His — not mine!' cut in Adam, no trace of humour in voice or eyes now. 'I'm heir to it, but I don't want it. Never did. You can't understand that any more than Father does, can you?

'I made a fortune in India and had a *very* good life there — I'm not about to spend the next forty years trotting back and forth from Akenside running a pot-works!'

'Father will *never* agree to your selling Whitlock's!'

'You think not?' he countered smoothly. 'Despite his sentiment about the works, our father is a shrewd man of business. He'll recognise Parkers' offer as one far too good to refuse.'

'You're *wrong!*'

'Am I indeed?' Draining his glass and rising, Adam swept up the correspondence and, brushing past Penelope, strode out into the hallway toward the staircase. 'I'm about to prove there's *no* sentiment in business!'

'Leave us for a bit, will you, lass?'

Penelope had no choice but to respect Elias's request and do as she was bidden. She'd hurriedly followed Adam upstairs. Now, she trailed down again to wait in her sitting-room, praying her father would not be distressed and his recovery suffer a setback, and blaming herself for forcing Adam's hand.

'Father wants to see you.'

Penelope started violently, springing to her feet and rushing past Adam up to her father's room. To her immense relief, Elias appeared well and perfectly composed, seated with the Parker & Sons' correspondence neatly stacked upon the table beside him.

'The pottery'll not be sold, Penny.' He looked up at her. 'Mind, it's a sterling offer! Parkers' are a canny firm. Cotton manufacturers. Adam struck a hard bargain. Couldn't have done better myself — I see now why the lad did so well for himself in India!'

Penelope stared at Elias incredulously. 'You sound as though you *admire* Adam!'

'I *do* admire him. If this offer came from a potter who'd keep on our people, I'd give the sale my blessing! As is, Parkers' have no use for pot-workers and I'll not be responsible for turning out our own folk and robbing them of their livelihoods.'

'You really would have sold Whitlock's?' She shook her head in disbelief. 'I don't understand, Father. The pottery means everything to you!'

'Aye, it does — but not to Adam,' he replied sadly, drawing a measured breath. 'I've been thinking back, Penny. My father was a miner, from a long line of miners. Da expected me to follow him down the pit — but I was having none of it! Soon as I got old enough, I upped sticks and went to Liverpool — '

'That was different, Father!' chipped in Penelope, wishing to comfort him. 'The pottery belongs to our *family*! To be passed down to Adam and — '

'He's determined to go his own way, lass. Didn't I do the same when I was young?' finished Elias, adding with a rueful smile, 'Happen Adam is more like me than he knows!'

★　★　★

'Here we are, Am!' cried Dorcas proudly, elbowing her in the ribs when their carriage turned into a terrace of imposing residences. '*This* is Rishton Place!'

Amaryllis had never been to Castlebridge before, but was denied any opportunity of pausing to admire the sights in the old Roman town because Dorcas had insisted upon their driving directly to her new home. The matched pair of high-stepping, sleek black carriage horses slowed to a halt and the women alighted.

'Our stables, carriage-house and quarters for the coachman and groom are at the rear,' Dorcas was saying, starting up a broad flight of steps towards the front door.

To Amaryllis's left, alongside these steps, was an ornately-wrought railing with a gate leading down to a low door and a little basement window. 'Is that part of your house?'

'Servants' and tradesmen's entrance,' replied Dorcas. 'The kitchen, wine cellar and so on. Our cook, house-keeper and butler have their rooms down there, too. The maids' accommodation is in the attics.'

Amaryllis gazed upwards. This was the tallest building she'd ever seen! At the very top, a row of attics had small windows, but rooms on the remaining three storeys had large, long windows with — how many? — nine, twelve, *eighteen* square panes.

'The library and Adam's study are on this floor, and *this* is my morning-room.' Dorcas swept across the entrance hall, indicating a prettily decorated room. 'It's where I receive visitors. I already have a circle of genteel ladies calling upon me.'

Amaryllis started into the attractive room, but her sister was already on the staircase.

'I must show you the drawing-room! The flock wallpaper was terribly expensive — you wouldn't believe wallpaper could cost so much! — but as Adam says, it *is* the very height of fashion and exquisite taste!' She turned along the first floor landing into a large, L-shaped room with a pianoforte in one corner. 'After dinner, we ladies retire here and leave the gentlemen in the dining-room to their port, cigars and conversation!

'We frequently entertain dinner guests. Many are members of Adam's club. Simon Baldwin dines regularly here. Adam regards him a fine fellow, and they are the closest of friends.' Dorcas paused, considering her younger sister sceptically. 'You were a fool letting Simon Baldwin go, Am! You'll never get anybody else of his calibre to — '

'Is Adam at home?' chipped in

Amaryllis pleasantly, keen to shift the subject.

'He's in York on business. He'll be gone until the day after tomorrow. This is the dining-room,' she went on, flinging open double-doors leading into an altogether more masculine room. 'Next month, Adam and I are having our very first formal dinner party! The absolute *cream* of Lancashire society will be attending. Cook and I are already planning menus. She's a splendid cook: far superior to that awful old woman they have at Haddonsell Grange!' Dorcas wrinkled her nose. 'Adam says an excellent cook is more precious than pearls, and — '

Amaryllis's head was spinning by the time they reached the third floor.

'Adam is *such* a generous husband. Wait until you see what he's had delivered for me today! I've already sent for my dressmaker and milliner,' laughed Dorcas, catching Amaryllis's arm and ushering her through the sumptuous master bedroom into an adjoining lady's sitting-room where several packages lay, their contents spilling out in a kalidoescope of brightly-coloured and hand-painted chinz, pastel-striped ginghams, floral sprigged muslins, and fresh white cotton, silk and lace.

'Everything is obviously the most exquisite quality.' Dipping into one of the packages, Dorcas withdrew lengths of material, allowing the shimmering folds to tumble across her outstretched arms. 'But just *look* at these glorious silks, Am —

'And did you ever see such delicate lace — it's lighter than gossamer!'

Early next morning, Noah Pendleton brought The Bell's flour from his family's mill and helped Sandy heft the sacks indoors. Pausing before clambering onto the heavy mill-cart, he stood gazing along the beach to where Amaryllis was seaweeding.

'If you've time,' Sandy called from the water-pump, 'go and try cheering the lass up a bit!'

Noah turned sharply. 'Why? What's wrong?'

Sandy shook his head, bewildered. 'Yesterday, she went over to visit Dorcas at Rishton Place. We've hardly had a word out of her since she got back.'

Noah lost no time joining Amaryllis foraging along the pools and rocks of the high shore; the tenderest plants were used for stews and soups, the rest to nourish the soil of the inn's kitchen garden.

'Is it true that ordinary, honest folk,' she began at length, repeating the very words Simon Baldwin had once used, 'people like parsons, doctors, school-teachers, shopkeepers and the like, have dealings with smugglers?'

'It's true that many folk buy contra-band,' replied Noah, considering his companion curiously. 'But most don't have any dealings with the smugglers themselves. Free-trading is a chain with lots of links, Amaryllis. Folk buy their goods from a middleman.'

'Such as a-friend-of-a-friend who

knows somebody,' she pondered, frowning.

'What's this about?' he queried quietly. 'Have you seen — or heard — something about what's been going on up-coast?'

Amaryllis shook her head vigorously, explanations coming in a rush. 'I visited Dorcas yesterday. Adam's bought her lots of material for dresses — chintz, muslins, gingham, all sorts — but there were lengths of *silk* too, Noah! Silk, and the very finest lace!

'Dorcas told me Adam and Simon Baldwin are close friends and Simon's frequently at Rishton Place. What if . . . ' She broke off.

Noah was no longer listening. His eyes were narrowed, staring far away along the low shore.

There was something, someone — even from this distance, there could be no doubt it was a person washing up into the shallows of the spent tide.

Noah was racing down over the wet sand, lest there be a chance the poor soul could be saved.

Amaryllis ran after him, slowing when she saw Noah drop to his knees at the water's edge; the lifeless figure sprawled before him amidst gently lapping saltwater.

She rested a comforting hand upon Noah's shoulder, feeling his whole body shudder. Slowly, Noah raised his face and looked up into her eyes.

'This man didn't drown, Amaryllis — he's been *murdered*!'

8

During the darkness of a hot summer's night, merchantman *Wilhelmina*, bound for her home port of Liverpool, was wrecked north of Macgregor's Cove and her valuable cargo pillaged.

Come morning, Amaryllis Macgregor and Noah Pendleton discovered a lifeless stranger upon the sands; but his were not the only remains to be borne ashore during that day, nor to be washed up amongst the breakers of subsequent tides.

'Soldiers found the makings of the false light that drew *Wilhelmina* in to shallow water and broke her over Gibbett Rocks,' Sandy Macgregor was relating when he called at Haddonsell Grange the following evening. 'There'd been passengers as well as crew aboard.

'Them as didn't drown were *mur-dered*, Elias! Cut down as they struggled ashore. Every last one of 'em stripped of their valuables.'

'I hear tell there were women on board?' queried Elias Whitaker, his haggard face bleak. 'They too perished?'

'We found them at the foot of the rocks,' Sandy answered, getting to his feet and striding over to the window. It was flung wide, for it had been another hot, still day. He stared down across the tranquil beauty of Elias's flower gardens, roughly rubbing a coarse hand across the stubble on his jaw.

He'd barely slept since Am and Noah found that first body. Him, Iain, Kit and Noah Pendleton, together with other menfolk from the cove, had taken responsibility for fetching up the dead from the beach before bearing them in waggons to the church of St. Agnes where they lay, awaiting naming and burial.

'Those two women.' Clearing his throat, Sandy turned from the window and went back to his seat facing Elias

Whitlock. 'They were the captain's wife and her widowed sister. Even their gold wedding bands had been taken off their fingers. It was a horrible thing to see, Elias. Horrible.'

The elderly man pushed a generous tot of rum toward his old friend, and Sandy Macgregor downed it gratefully.

'We've had *Wilhelmina*'s owner up from Liverpool today,' he went on grimly. 'Man called Protheroe. I don't like the cut of him at all. He's staying at The Bell. Marched right in, asking questions. Demanding to see everything. Kit took him up to the church. It was Protheroe put names to the two ladies. And to the body Am and Noah found.

'He was a Dutchman,' finished Sandy, frowning. 'But it's queer, y'know. *Wilhelmina*'s entire cargo was plundered, yet the only thing Protheroe quizzed Am and Noah about is them finding the Dutchman. He's asked them over and over if they're *sure* they saw none of his belongings nearby. I reckon that Dutchman must've been carrying summat particular, and Protheroe wants it back bad.'

'Happen you're right,' opined Elias shrewdly. 'If the Dutchman was his agent — carrying who knows what — then small wonder Protheroe's posted a hefty reward for capture of the wreckers!'

'The brass'd be better spent investing in Kit's lighthouse. A permanent light would make this coast safer all round.' Sandy rose wearily, taking his battered hat from a highly-polished plum-wood table.

'*Wilhelmina*'s cargo and whatever the Dutchman carried are long gone, Elias — long gone. Like the thieves and murderers who lured that vessel and every soul aboard her to their graves!'

* * *

'After apple-picking!' replied Penelope, beaming at Kit as they rode from

265

Haddonsell Grange through sun-baked sandy lanes out toward The Bell. 'It was Betsy's idea.

'We were all together at the inn-house, and I'd just asked Amaryllis and Betsy if they'd be my bridesmaids. Ethel said it was high time you and I set a date, and that's when Betsy suggested — '

'Apple-picking!' laughed Kit, reaching across the distance between their horses to catch hold of her fingers. 'Sounds perfect!'

'I think so,' agreed Penelope contentedly. 'September's a beautifully warm, golden month — lovely for a wedding!'

It was to be a quiet, old-fashioned wedding at the little church of St. Agnes. Upon this, the couple were already decided.

Riding at a leisurely pace and conversing about their future plans, Penelope and Kit reached The Bell as the mail coach was departing.

Alerted to their approach by Flossie, Betsy immediately raced across the cobbles brandishing a couple of letters and carrying a laden fruit basket.

'What have the pair of you been gathering, Betsy?' asked Penelope, bending to fuss Flossie and peek into the trug. 'Oh, my — they're beauties!'

'I know. We're baking a big gooseberry tart for supper.'

'May I help?'

'You can help Ammie and me top-and-tail the goosegogs while Ma makes pastry,' nodded Betsy. Turning her attention to Kit, she held out one of the letters. 'This is yours. The other is for Ammie. It's from Dorcas, I recognise her writing. It's funny though, because Ammie *never* gets letters!'

With that, child and dog were off, running toward the inn-house.

'I'll tell Ma and Ammie you're here, Penny!' Betsy called over her shoulder. 'We'll be in the kitchen!'

Smiling, Penelope turned to Kit — and her smiled faded. He was quite still; his head was bowed, and he was staring at the letter.

267

'Kit?' she whispered. 'Whatever is it?'

'It's from Jamaica,' he murmured, looking up. 'Tabby's reply.'

Penelope touched a gentle hand to his arm. 'I'll see to the horses while you read her letter.'

Taking both reins, she led Patch and Sorrel across the cobbled yard towards the stables. Kit spoke often and with deepest affection of Tabitha Warburton, and Penelope was aware the elderly Jamaican woman had been part of his life for as long as he could recall. It was indeed probable, as Kit had reasoned, that the only person able to answer his questions concerning Marietta and how he came to be brought up as a Chesterton *was* Tabby . . .

When she emerged a little while later from the stables, Penelope found Kit sitting on the edge of the stone horse trough, the open letter resting loosely within both his hands. She sat beside him and, wordlessly, he offered Tabby's letter.

Taking hold of Kit's hand, Penelope

began reading the painstakingly neat, old-fashioned writing. Warmth and love shone from every word, as did Tabby's devotion for the Chesterton family, and especially for Clara: the mistress to whom, Penelope knew, Tabby had been lady's maid, friend and companion since both were young girls.

Clara had always loved children and longed for a family, read Penelope. After years of hoping, her son Geoffrey was born, but it was a difficult birth and doctors told her she would never bear another child.

You won't remember my sister Bathsheba, wrote Tabby, *she was a laundress down in Jobert Town.*

When Geoffrey was almost two years old, fever broke out in Jobert and many, many people were dying. Bathsheba wrote me that her friend Marietta had perished but Marietta's infant son still lived. Bathsheba wanted to get you away from the town to somewhere safe where there was no fever.

She brought you up here to Florence

and came to the villa. She asked me to go with her to the orphanage and beg them to take you in — but your mama overheard Bathsheba and me talking. Before she even set eyes on you, that sweet lady said you'd be going nowhere, because you were already home.

And that's how you came to be family, child . . .

'It's a beautiful letter,' Penelope raised her eyes from the page and looked at Kit, wishing they were alone so she might hold him close. 'Written with great love!'

He nodded, drawing a deep, measured breath, 'One day, Penny, when time and our work permit, you and I must sail for Jamaica and visit my old home in Florence. I want you to meet my family, and get to know Tabby, Geoffrey and Susan.'

'I'd like that very much, my dearest,' responded Penelope, a catch in her voice.

Kit leaned across to kiss her cheek. 'Betsy will be waiting for you to help top-and-tailing those goosegogs,' he murmured with a slow smile, his gaze once more returning to Tabitha Warburton's letter.

'I need to show this to Sandy.'

* * *

The family supper at the inn-house had long since been eaten and cleared before Amaryllis remembered the letter from Dorcas.

She'd hurriedly pushed it into the pocket of her apron when Betsy had brought it in, and been kept far too busy doing chores to give it another thought until she was undressing for bed. Amaryllis felt the letter as she untied her apron and withdrawing it from the pocket, was sorely tempted to set it aside until morning.

It'd been another long day; a deal of it taken up by *Wilhelmina*'s owner Protheroe asking her yet more questions about the finding of the murdered Dutchman. Amaryllis was weary, but conscience wouldn't allow her to ignore the letter.

Mindful of disturbing Betsy's sleep, Amaryllis crept from the room they shared out onto the landing and lit a candle there. Sitting on the top stair, she opened Dorcas's letter and was startled by the opening lines.

Burn this the moment you've read it, Am! Whatever you do, don't let Ma or Pa see it.

When Ma came to Rishton Place yesterday she insisted on coming back on Wednesday to help me with new curtains. I told her it wasn't necessary — I have servants to do such things — but I just could not put her off!

Mrs Stanley Lockwood and her daughters are giving me the favour of calling upon me on Wednesday. The Lockwoods are of the highest quality, Am. I can't possibly have Ma here when they come! I'm relying on you to devise a plan for keeping her away —

Amaryllis broke off in indignation. Dorcas was beyond belief!

Distractedly skimming the following paragraphs, Amaryllis paused with a jolt. Her sister was writing proudly about an invitation to a summer ball at the country estate belonging to one of Adam's old school friends . . .

Nicholas Fenwick is a captain or major or some such high rank, and has command of the Castlebridge Garrison.

His family are among the grandest in Lancashire, and Adam promised to present me with something special to wear at the Fenwick ball. As you know, I've no patience with surprises, so when Adam was away in Chester I went into his dressing-room and happened to look in the tall-boy and there amongst his shirts was the most glorious necklace!

Huge diamonds and sapphires, Am! It fairly took my breath away and must be worth a king's ransom. It's certainly fit for a queen! The ladies at that summer ball will be green with envy.

With a rush, Amaryllis's long-held suspicion that Adam Whitlock regularly purchased contraband engulfed her.

Unbidden, the persistent questions *Wilhelmina*'s owner had asked concerning the Dutchman — together with Noah's reckoning he might've been a goldsmith, gem merchant or some such from Amsterdam — flooded her mind.

Amaryllis's blood ran cold.

Dismissing her notions as wild and fanciful, she held Dorcas's letter to the candle flame and watched it burn into ashes. But not so easily could Amaryllis rid herself of a shocking speculation.

Was Dorcas's diamond necklace *plunder* from the wrecked merchantman?

★　★　★

'By, this is the happiest birthday I've ever had, our Penny!' sighed Dorothy Whitlock contentedly.

It was late afternoon and they were on the terrace overlooking the gardens at Haddonsell, putting the finishing touches to a table set with the delicate, floral-patterned and gilded *Dorothy* tea service.

Following her mother's gaze, Penelope watched Kit strolling with her father seated in his new wheeled chair. It was the first time for more than a year Elias had been outdoors to his beloved gardens.

'I don't like thinking back to my last birthday, and how ill he was then,' went on Dorothy softly, glancing up at Penelope. 'I thought we were going to lose him — and now look! Your father's back where he belongs among his flowers and his bees, and the pair of you have made this grand tea-set for me!'

'It was Father's idea from long ago,' smiled Penelope. 'We've already started throwing the line in earnest and are taking plenty of orders. I do believe the *Dorothy* will be one of our most popular tea-sets!'

'It *is* lovely,' murmured Dorothy, admiring the clear, brilliant glaze of the richly hand-painted creamware. 'We're having a right gradely day, aren't we? It's a shame Adam and Dorcas couldn't come, but I daresay they have their own affairs to see to.'

'I'm truly sorry Adam chose to quit the pottery,' Penelope said after a moment. 'If only I hadn't confronted him as I did! If I'd *waited* . . . Perhaps, given time, Adam might've had a change of heart and decided against selling out — '

'Nay, lass — it wasn't your fault,' cut in Dorothy firmly. 'You're not to blame; neither is Adam. He is who he is. You can't fit a square peg into a round hole. Adam was bound to go his own way again sooner or later — and why shouldn't he?

'He's never had a care for Whitlock's or the estate,' she went on matter-of-factly. 'It were *you* always asking questions and wanting to learn about the pot-works and Haddonsell.'

'Watter's boiling and I'm warming the pot,' said Nora Mumford, the Grange's cook, poking her head around the door onto the terrace. 'If they want to drink their tea hot, you'd best call in the menfolk and get 'em sat round the table — for I'm bringing it in directly!'

★   ★   ★

The little party made short work of Mrs Mumford's feather-light cakes, melting pastries and moreish dainties and were lingering over third cups of tea when a maid appeared bearing Cyril Protheroe's card.

'He said he's on his way back to Liverpool, sir,' she explained, giving the card to Kit. 'They told him at The Bell you'd be here, and he wants to see you most urgent.'

Unimpressed, Kit considered the card and glanced around the table to Penelope and her parents.

'Protheroe is among the wealthiest shipowners I've approached,' he remarked drily. 'In common with the others, he agreed the construction of a lighthouse was a worthy endeavour —

then promptly showed me the door!'

'I've never met Cyril Protheroe, but I've *heard* plenty about him!' remarked Elias thoughtfully. 'He's a man with his thumb in lots of pies, Kit. It's no secret he has political ambitions and is fixing to be next Mayor of Liverpool. Lately, he's been taking up charitable works and good causes around the town. Fancies himself summat of a *philan-thropist*, by all accounts.'

'Does he now?' mused Kit, rising from the tea-table. 'Maybe our Mr Protheroe is having second thoughts about investing in a lighthouse . . . '

*   *   *

Dorcas Whitlock arrived at The Bell in a flurry of anger and impatience.

At her insistence, the carriage-man had driven from Rishton Place with near reckless speed and almost before he'd let down the step, Dorcas alighted the vehicle, striding toward the inn as Mathilda Macgregor was emerging from the inn-house with Betsy and Flossie.

'Great Aunt!' she called across the yard. 'Where's my sister?'

'And a good day to you, too, Dorcas!' returned Mathilda crisply. 'How nice of you to come calling — '

Dorcas was no longer listening. Sweeping up the steps, she entered the inn and found Amaryllis kneeling on the floor with a basket of small brushes, rags, polishing cloths and dishes of wax at her side.

Making the most of a lull in comings-and-goings at The Bell, Amaryllis had set to cleaning the hearthside carved-oak settle. Glancing up at sound of quick footsteps ringing upon the stone flags, she was astonished to see Dorcas — who hadn't set foot in Macgregor's Cove since returning from her wedding trip.

'Am — you and I have never been close,' she began before Amaryllis could draw breath to greet her. 'And heaven knows, I wouldn't be here now if I had anybody else to turn to, but *you're* the only one I can tell — and you must never breathe a word of this. I will not be publicly humiliated and made to look a fool!'

'Whatever's wrong?' exclaimed Amaryllis, not unduly concerned: Dorcas was prone to exaggerated outbursts.

'*This!*'

She flung a slender, glittering bracelet down onto the bundle of rags and polishing cloths.

'Adam promised me a special present to wear at the Fenwick summer ball! And this — this *trinket* — is what he gave me!'

'It's very pretty,' commented Amaryllis, at a loss to understand her sister's agitation.

'*It's very pretty*,' mimicked Dorcas harshly. 'It isn't my exquisite diamond and sapphire necklace though, is it?'

'Well, no, but — '

'After Adam went out this morning, I searched every inch of his dressing-room — *and* his study,' she cut in, her green eyes bright with anger. 'There's no sign of my necklace anywhere!

'Where is it, Am? Who's he given it to?'

Amaryllis's jaw dropped. 'Surely you can't believe — '

'Don't be so naïve!' sneered Dorcas bitterly. 'Adam's given *my* necklace to another woman. Married gentlemen take mistresses — it's the way of the world. But I'm one wife who will not be sniggered about; nor will I be made a laughing-stock in society.

'I intend finding out exactly who the baggage is — and putting a stop to Adam's dalliances once and for all!'

★   ★   ★

'Flossie and I will miss you,' Betsy was saying, perched on the corner of the high bed in Kit's room at The Bell and watching him pack a small valise. 'Penny, too.'

'We'll only be gone three days,' he smiled, gently tugging one of the little girl's plaits. He and Penelope were attending Lydia Unsworth's wedding over at Skilbeck. 'And Yorkshire isn't so far away — '

Turning at a soft tap upon the open door, Kit saw Ethel looking in.

'Is there anything you need before you set off?'

'No, thanks.' He smiled and snapped shut the valise. 'I'm ready to go. If I *have* forgotten something, I'll just have to manage without it!'

'There's usually something gets left behind.' Returning his smile, Ethel began a shade hesitantly, 'With your brother being in Jamaica, have you chosen a best man for your wedding yet?'

'Hadn't even *thought* about it!' exclaimed Kit in consternation.

'Then why don't you ask Sandy? You're his only son, and it'd mean the world to him to be standing with you on your wedding day,' went on Ethel warmly. With a little bob of her head, she added, 'He'd like that very much, Kit — very much indeed!'

★ ★ ★

'Father organised it while Kit and I were in Yorkshire for Lydia's wedding,' laughed Penelope, glancing sidelong at Amaryllis. She'd been driving to The Bell with pots of Haddonsell's blossom honey when she met Amaryllis walking home from St. Agnes. 'The morning after we returned and I went to the pottery, there was a newly-painted sign above the gates: *Whitlock & Daughter, Master Potters!*

'I could hardly believe my eyes!' she reflected softly. 'Kit, Mother and Father, and all the pot-workers were there waiting for me in the yard. Everybody clapped and cheered as I rode in. It was — well — it was really touching.'

'You deserve it, Penny!' exclaimed Amaryllis. 'I think it's grand! And when I was in the book shop, Great Aunt was telling the vicar's wife that your taking over the family firm and running that pottery single-handed is an example and inspiration to all we womenfolk — '

She broke off as the chaise drew to a halt alongside the inn-house and Ethel hailed her from the kitchen garden.

'You've a message from Dorcas!' Ethel called, dusting earth from her hands. 'A lad come with it — it's on the mantle-shelf.'

Amaryllis hurriedly led the way indoors and unfolded the note, alarmed as she began reading. Dorcas had followed Adam! He'd taken private rooms at an establishment called Thornton's Hotel. She hadn't seen his mistress yet, but was —

'Not bad news, I hope?'

Amaryllis faltered. 'Lately, Dorcas has been . . . *worried*.'

'Is my brother the cause?' asked Penelope bluntly. At once, she added, 'Forgive me — I didn't intend prying!'

'You're not!' she frowned. 'In truth, I've no idea what to *do* about this note!'

'I'll gladly take you to Castlebridge,' offered the older woman. 'If you want to visit Dorcas?'

While Penelope was driving to Castlebridge, she and Amaryllis conversed about her wedding, the dresses they were making, Ethel's plans for baking the marriage cake, and a deal of everyday concerns. However, not until the chaise turned into Rishton Place did they speak about the purpose for their visit.

'Are you sure you aren't coming in?'

'It's best you see Dorcas on your own,' opined Penelope practically, drawing to a halt a carriage-length from the Whitlocks' imposing residence. A young groom was waiting directly outside, holding the bridle of his master's favourite bay. 'I'll do some errands and call back later.'

Amaryllis was approaching the front door when it was wrenched open, a cacophony of angry voices spilling out.

In horror, Penelope watched her brother marching furiously from the vestibule, almost knocking Amaryllis aside.

Muttering a startled apology, Adam Whitlock strode from the house. Dorcas was on the threshold, her eyes bright with rage and spots of hard colour staining her cheeks. Her acrimonious words disintegrated into sobs.

'What's going on here, Adam?' demanded Penelope, stepping into his path before he reached the waiting horse. 'Dorcas is distraught!'

'None of your concern,' he retorted brusquely, snatching the reins and dismissing the groom with a cursory wave of his hand. 'Make yourself useful by ensuring Dorcas doesn't follow me!'

'Why would your wife wish to follow you?' queried Penelope suspiciously.

'What I'm about is dangerous,' he confided unexpectedly. 'Quite by chance, it came to my hearing that the ringleaders behind the smuggling at the cove and the wrecking of *Wilhelmina* are regular card players at the King's Arms on Mount Pleasant.

'I've taken rooms at the hotel opposite and have been keeping a watchful eye upon various comings and goings at the tavern, its neighbouring carter's yards, store-house and livery stables,' continued Adam. 'There are few better methods of transporting contraband to customers than aboard waggons, drays and pack-horses loaded with legitimate goods!' he added drily.

Penelope considered her younger brother shrewdly. 'Why haven't you taken this intelligence to the garrison?'

'I can't. Not yet. Gerrard is one of the card-players — along with Simon Baldwin and a Manx fisherman — but Gerrard is my friend, Pen! He once risked his own life to save mine.

'I owe him the benefit of doubt,' reasoned Adam soberly. 'I won't call in the military until I'm absolutely certain Gerrard is involved.'

'This is not only dangerous, it's foolhardy!' argued Penelope, concern for her younger brother sharpening her tone. 'If those men suspect you're spying — '

'Don't worry about me, old girl — all

will be well!' Adam glanced down at her from the bay's saddle, his impetuous grin broad and confident. 'This time, I'm on the side of angels!'

★ ★ ★

Once indoors, Penelope explained in few words.

'I was wrong about him!' gasped Dorcas tearfully, relief rapidly becoming fear. 'But what if Adam gets hurt?'

'Has he told the garrison?' chipped in Amaryllis quickly.

Penelope shook her head, quitting the morning-room. 'But *I* intend doing so immediately!'

'I'll come with you, Penny.'

'Adam's *my* husband. Neither of you are going anywhere without me,' snapped Dorcas, reaching for the bell-pull. 'I'll have Groves bring around the carriage — '

'We've no time to lose; the sooner this is done, the better,' Penelope called from the hallway. 'We'll use the chaise!'

288

'When we get there, ask for Captain Fenwick,' responded Dorcas, hurrying after her. 'I met him at the summer ball — he's one of Adam's oldest friends.'

* * *

The sun was dipping in the west, and long shadows were falling across the castle battlements when the three women emerged from their interview with Captain Nicholas Fenwick.

'Penelope, it was exceedingly rude of you to refuse the captain's gallant suggestion of an officer to escort us to Rishton Place,' admonished Dorcas, stepping into the chaise. 'I'm certain he was offended!'

'Given everything we told him about Adam's suspicions, he surely has far more pressing concerns,' responded Penelope tartly, glancing over her shoulder as twelve mounted and heavily-armed redcoats thundered from the garrison.

'Besides, we aren't going directly to

Rishton Place.' Taking up the reins, she released the chaise's brake. 'We're following the soldiers.'

Turning into Mount Pleasant, she slowed the vehicle to a crawl, manoeuvring through a jostling, gathering crowd toward the King's Arms.

Musket-bearing redcoats were marching four men in chains from the tavern to the gaol-waggon awaiting them.

'*Adam!*'

Dorcas scrambled from the chaise before her companions could restrain her. But Penelope was at her heels, catching up with Dorcas and holding her fast, preventing her from flinging herself at the phalanx of armed soldiers guarding the prisoners in a desperate bid to reach her husband.

'Take her to Haddonsell!' Adam Whitlock's handsome face contorted with fury as he twisted around in the waggon, yelling at his sister. 'And *stay* there!'

★ ★ ★

'Adam Whitlock turned up at the Grange as though naught was amiss?' exclaimed Noah in disbelief next morning.

Amaryllis nodded, her shoulders bowed to the task of rowing-up, raking and rowing-up again the precious hay-crop in the long field beyond The Bell.

'It was getting late. Penny had taken us to Haddonsell and we'd explained to Mr and Mrs Whitlock about what happened at the King's Arms. Dorcas was inconsolable. She was complaining of a dreadful headache so Mrs Whitlock fixed her a soothing tincture. Dorcas was retiring when Adam arrived.

'He said being arrested was a storm in a teacup!' Straightening up, she pushed a stray strand of damp hair neatly beneath her faded calico bonnet. 'Adam told us since he was with the three suspects in the tavern, the redcoats naturally arrested him too. Once at the garrison, the misunderstanding was speedily resolved and he was released with profuse apologies from Captain Fenwick.'

'While the other three remain locked up in Castlebridge gaol awaiting trial for a capital offence,' commented Noah, shouldering a pitch and striding along lines of drying, golden hay. 'We'd had neither smuggling nor wrecking along our coast for twenty-odd years until Whitlock came back. I reckon he's not only up to his neck in what's been going on, but it's him giving the orders!'

Amaryllis spun around, staring at him in horror.

While convinced Adam Whitlock *was* guilty of purchasing contraband, she couldn't bring herself to believe her sister's husband was a smuggler, and responsible for *Wilhelmina*'s wrecking with the loss of all those aboard her!

'I've never liked Adam, but no! No, surely what you say cannot be,' she reasoned quietly. 'He was *spying* on those men, Noah. Why would he do that if they were in cahoots?'

'Maybe there'd been a falling out amongst thieves, or the others were getting greedy and Whitlock suspected them of taking more than their share of profits,' speculated Noah with a shrug. 'All we know for certain is Whitlock, Simon Baldwin, Gerrard and Killip were together at the King's Arms when the redcoats got there.

'We only have his word about everything else — and I wouldn't trust Adam Whitlock as far as I could throw him!'

The two old friends laboured on throughout the morning, speaking little. It was almost dinnertime when Sandy strode past the field to meet an incoming mail coach.

'Thanks for offering to help with the hay, Noah!' he called, squinting up at the blue, cloudless sky. 'We need to get it in before this weather breaks!'

He'd no sooner gone on his way than he was back again, sticking his head around the hedgerow and shouting.

''News just come with the coach

— them as Adam put in gaol escaped during the night! Like as not bribed the turn-key, I reckon.

'Redcoats killed two of 'em making a run for it,' Sandy went on, hurrying back toward the inn's yard. 'T'other one — him who was baillie up at the Grange — got clean away!'

★   ★   ★

The August afternoon was warm and balmy, and Dorothy Whitlock was putting on a bit of a family get-together in the gardens at Haddonsell to bid farewell and godspeed to Adam and Dorcas.

It was a perfect day for one of Mrs Mumford's substantial picnics and afterwards, in their twos and threes, the party gradually drifted away to stroll the shady riverbank, linger amongst the fragrant flower gardens, or find a comfortable spot to sit and make most of the late summer sunshine.

Dorothy and Ethel plumped for

settling down on the terrace with their workbaskets and fresh cups of tea.

'When Adam came home from India last year,' reflected Dorothy, 'I never thought he'd up-sticks and be off again so soon! 'Specially with him and Dorcas only newly wed.'

'I know,' agreed Ethel, taking out her knitting. 'And fancy giving up that beautiful house of theirs in Rishton Place! All this came right out of the blue, too. When Dorcas told us and I asked her where they were going, she said they hadn't decided yet!

'She said they wanted to travel and see the world. Have you ever heard the like?'

Dorothy turned to her companion. 'Do you think they'll ever come back, Ethel? Come home again, I mean?'

'Eee, I don't know,' She sighed, looking across the gardens to her beautiful, accomplished daughter. These past few weeks, Ethel hadn't been able to quell the dread that she might never see Dorcas again, nor ever see the grandchildren who would surely come along in time. 'We've no say in the matter, have we?'

With a shake of her head, Dorothy too gazed out upon the garden, to the furthest corner and the old swing beneath the great horse chestnut tree.

'Adam loved that swing when he was a little lad,' she murmured wistfully, adding with a small smile. 'It's nice seeing somebody swinging on it again!'

★   ★   ★

'Why aren't Dorcas and Adam staying for Kit and Penny's wedding?' asked Betsy, stretched out beneath the horse chestnut's great, leafy umbrella.

Amaryllis slid from the swing and dropped down onto the grass beside her young sister before replying. 'I expect they're impatient to set off on their travels.'

'They don't even know where they're going!' declared Betsy indignantly. 'Kit and Penny have decided to go to

Scotland on *their* trip!'

Amaryllis tried to look aghast. 'They're not secretly eloping to Gretna Green, are they?'

'Of course not!' laughed Betsy. 'Ages ago, Penny asked me to tell her the story of how in the olden days our family came from a Scottish village to Macgregor's Cove and I showed her the map I'd drawn of their journey.

'She and Kit are travelling by road up to the village and staying in Scotland for their honeymoon, afterwards they'll *sail* down to the cove exactly like the very first Macgregors did!'

★ ★ ★

'Kit's asked me to be his best man,' Sandy remarked, offering his baccy pouch to Elias.

'Aye, Penny said. You and me'll need to smarten ourselves up,' He grinned, helping himself to the strong, dark tobacco. 'Best bib-and-tucker for the big day!'

'Are you alright going this far?' queried Sandy. They'd left the garden and were walking at snail's pace through Haddonsell's woodland. 'It's a long way.'

'Now I can get out under my own steam,' returned Elias, indicating his stout hazel-wood stick. 'I make the most of it!'

Sandy nodded, lighting his pipe. 'How's work on the canal going?'

'We reckon it'll be finished early next year,' replied the elderly man proudly. With a broad grin, he added, 'Then that lad of yours'll be full speed ahead building his lighthouse!'

'A permanent light can't come soon enough to the cove,' Sandy commented soberly. 'God willing, we've heard the inn's tolling bell ring out for the last time, Elias — too many lives have already been lost.'

At length, they turned, slowly retracing their path back through the wood.

'We were right about that Dutchman aboard the *Wilhelmina* carrying summat particular,' related Elias breathlessly, leaning heavily on the hazel-wood stick. 'Yesterday, an old pal from Liverpool visited me. He's very thick with Cyril Protheroe.

'Harry told me Protheroe commissioned a jeweller in Amsterdam to make a necklace for his wife. That's what the Dutchman was bringing to Liverpool — a diamond necklace, with sapphires big as robins' eggs.'

* * *

On the morning of her marriage, Penelope rose and dressed hours before the household stirred, slipping out for her daily walk.

Starting across the garden, she caught sight of Kit sitting beneath the lime, his back leaning against the greyish ridged bark and his hat drawn down over his eyes.

'Have you been here all night?'

'Feels like it.' He rose stiffly, flexing his shoulders. 'I wanted to see you

299

before our wedding, Penny. Be with you. Is that alright?'

She kissed him, and smiled. 'That's alright.'

At The Bell, Ethel had forbidden anybody to go near the inn-house pantry, lest some mishap befall the richly fruited, marzipanned and daintily-decorated Lancashire marriage cake before it was presented to the newly-wed couple.

She and the other womenfolk — Sandy and Iain had long-since made themselves scarce — were in a flurry of preparations when Betsy spotted Kit and Penelope down on the beach.

'They're never together today!' exclaimed Widow Watkins, making a beeline for the big bay window, closely followed by Ethel. 'Let's see — '

The far shore was swathed in drifting wisps of hazy September mist, the tide quietly ebbing, and with arms entwined, Penelope and Kit were meandering along the damp, shell-strewn sand.

'Not right, is it?' tutted Freda Watkins. 'And it's bad luck an' all, bride and groom seeing each other before the wedding!'

'Foolish superstition,' rebuked Ethel, frowning. 'It's not seemly, though, is it? Being down there together like that. Not *proper*.'

Amaryllis hadn't joined them at the window. She remained at the ironing-table, pressing Betsy's best ribbons; her mind brooding over a few lines from Dorcas's letter, which had arrived on the day's first coach.

We've taken a divine villa here and Adam arranged a most elegant party to celebrate my 21ˢᵗ birthday.

You'll never guess what he gave me, Am — a certain necklace! Adam must've kept it hidden away all these months as a surprise for my special birthday.

'Am, stop wool-gathering and finish pressing those ribbons — we've plenty more chores before we set off for church,' Ethel reprimanded, her stern expression softening when she glanced once more from the bay window.

'Kit and Penny make a lovely couple, don't they?'

★ ★ ★

The sisters had enjoyed a good day's fruit gathering at the St. Agnes ruins.

'We've left lots for the squirrels, wood-mice and birds to eat,' Amaryllis was saying when they emerged into bright golden sunlight from the medi-eval priory's shady beech wood, trugs heavy with curly-husked, glossy, brown nuts collected from beneath the huge old trees.

'It's good we got more crab-apples, too. We'll need them for our last jam-making of the season,' she went on, smiling down at Betsy. 'You did really well spotting that thicket of ripe blackberries!'

'*And* we've picked them before Michaelmas,' laughed Betsy, dipping into the basket and sampling one of the plump fruits. 'When the Devil throws his cloak over the berries and spoils them!'

Amaryllis laughed too, exclaiming, 'End of September already! The days since Kit and Penny's wedding have flown by — do you think they'll be in Scotland yet?'

Betsy shook her head, stooping to tease out a clump of burdock bracts tangled in Flossie's silky white fur. 'Kit told me they'll stay a while at that hotel where they went skating last winter. Penny's promised to sketch the lake for me — and lots of other sights too — so I can put them in my book with the Macgregors' map.'

With Flossie snuffing on ahead, the sisters started the lengthy walk homewards with their harvest of nuts, fruit and berries. Presently, the dunes gave way to caves and green cliffs. The breeze was freshening now, and the sun-spangled tide rolled in slow and quiet, its spume-fringed waves thumping softly upon the shore before rushing

303

back a little and leaving lacy patterns on the wet sand.

Amaryllis paused, gazing out to sea and drew a deep, contented breath.

'It's perfect for sailing. I'm really looking forward to our taking *Starfish* out today, Betsy! And I'm so glad Noah's able to come with us.

'Lately, whenever he isn't away skippering the packet, he's been occupied helping his father and brother at the mill so we've hardly seen him.' She sighed, unintentionally murmuring her thoughts aloud. 'I miss him.'

*   *   *

Approaching The Bell, Amaryllis felt a surge of happiness, smiling at sight of Noah Pendleton. He was on the beach, making ready *Starfish*.

As though sensing her gaze upon him, Noah turned from his work. Shielding his eyes from the sun, he looked up to see Amaryllis entering the inn's cobbled yard.

'Hurry up!' he called cheerfully. 'Time and tide wait for no one!'

'I know!' she returned, shifting the weight of the heavy trugs. 'We'll put this fruit away and be right out!'

With heart singing, Amaryllis headed toward the inn-house's kitchen door. She paid scant attention to Betsy making a beeline for the pump and drawing fresh water for Flossie; didn't notice Ethel scurrying from The Bell to have a few conspiratorial words with the child, and much less did she notice Betsy's delighted response and vigorous nodding.

In no time at all, beech nuts and crab-apples were safely stored away, while the ripe blackberries were left upon the pantry's cold marble shelf ready for jamming.

Absorbed in thoughts of Noah, Amaryllis sped across the cobbled yard toward the beach and didn't at first realise Betsy wasn't following her. Glancing back, she saw the little girl standing on the steps of The Bell,

Flossie at her side.

'Aren't you coming?' she cried in astonishment.

Beaming, Betsy shook her head. 'I want to stay here and help Ma make my blackberries into jam!'

'You *must* come with us, Betsy!' protested Amaryllis. 'It's a beautiful evening for sailing and — '

'Betsy will go next time,' chipped in Ethel firmly, joining her youngest daughter on the steps. 'Don't dawdle, Am — away you go! We'll stay here and wave you off!'

Leaving *Starfish* bobbing in the shallow surf, Noah sprinted across the sands to meet Amaryllis, his pleasure at seeing her undisguised. 'This is grand, us taking *Starfish* out together — I've really missed you, Amaryllis!'

Meeting his frank, appreciative eyes, of a sudden Amaryllis felt shy and awkward with her childhood pal. 'I've missed *you* more than I can say,' she faltered, rushing on. 'It seems ages since I last saw you and during the walk home, I told Betsy how very glad I was you were coming with us this evening.'

'Amaryllis . . . '

Softly breathing her name, Noah impulsively moved closer — and instantly drew back. Tearing his gaze from her upturned face, he stared far beyond Amaryllis to The Bell; to Betsy and Ethel standing there.

Clearing his throat, he asked, 'Isn't Betsy coming sailing?'

Amaryllis shook her head. 'She's making blackberry jam instead.'

'It's just us, then?'

'Yes.'

From their vantage point at The Bell, Ethel and Betsy had a clear view of Amaryllis and Noah Pendleton.

'It's been a long while happening,' Ethel remarked contentedly, her arm about the child's shoulders. 'But thanks be, happen it has — those two are a match made in heaven, Betsy!'

Curious, Sandy ambled over from the stables and joined them on the steps. 'What are you two smiling about?'

'Ammie and Noah!' beamed Betsy. '*Look*, Pa!'

The young couple were conversing quietly, walking so close their arms occasionally brushed. When Noah offered his hand, Amaryllis linked her fingers through his and together they wandered on down the gently sloping sandshore to *Starfish*.

Hoisting the sail, Amaryllis glanced sidelong up to The Bell; glimpsing her family, she raised an arm, waving joyously. Noah cast off, clambering aboard and taking his place beside her in the trim little craft.

Canvas billowed and *Starfish* ran before the fresh wind, catching the rush of a swift, high tide as Amaryllis and Noah sailed across the deep, clear water of Macgregor's Cove.

Ashore, Sandy Macgregor turned to his wife and wee daughter.

'Aye,' he nodded sagely. 'Happen the pair of you'll be baking another marriage cake afore we know it . . . '

We do hope that you have enjoyed reading this large print book.

Did you know that all of our titles are available for purchase?

We publish a wide range of high quality large print books including:
Romances, Mysteries, Classics
General Fiction
Non Fiction and Westerns

Special interest titles available in large print are:
The Little Oxford Dictionary
Music Book, Song Book
Hymn Book, Service Book

Also available from us courtesy of Oxford University Press:
Young Readers' Dictionary
(large print edition)
Young Readers' Thesaurus
(large print edition)

For further information or a free brochure, please contact us at:
Ulverscroft Large Print Books Ltd.,
The Green, Bradgate Road, Anstey,
Leicester, LE7 7FU, England.
Tel: (00 44) **0116 236 4325**
Fax: (00 44) **0116 234 0205**

Film-set director Evie is between projects, and hurting from being dumped by the arrogant Marcus. Escaping to spend Christmas in her parents' idyllic countryside home, what will finally lift her mood — her mum's relentless festive spirit, the cosiness of village traditions . . . or the attention of gorgeous antiques dealer Jake? When the leading duo in this year's village pantomime drops out after a bust-up, Evie and Jake are roped in to take over. But with Evie playing the princess, just how seriously will Jake take his new role as Prince Charming?

LOVING LADY SARAH

J. Darley

As life returns to normal after the war, Lady Sarah Trenton's reality is put into perspective. Her love for Robert, the gamekeeper's son who has returned home safely, is as alive as ever. But they must meet in secret, for Lord Trenton, whose heart has been hardened by the loss of his son, intends to see his daughter marry a man of wealth and status — like the odious Sir Percy. The times are changing, but the class divide is as wide as ever. Will Sarah and Robert be forced apart?

FORBIDDEN FLOWERS

Alice Elliott

An embarrassing slip in the Hyde Park mud leads Lily and Rose Banister into the path of Philip Montgomery, a British Embassy diplomat. Mesmerised by Lily's beauty, he invites her to accompany him to the Paris Exhibition, while Rose, who can't help but feel envious, is asked to chaperone the trip. Arriving in Paris, the trio happen upon Philip's old adversary Gordon Pomfret, who decides to join their group, obviously vying for Lily's attention. Meanwhile, Rose and Philip discover that their shared interests might just make them kindred spirits . . .

CLOSE TO THE EDGE

Sheila Spencer-Smith

Grieving the death of her brother, Alix decides to make a fresh start on the Dorset coast. Her new job, running the tearoom attached to Mellstone Gallery, comes with its own difficulties — not least the petulant attitude of her employer's daughter Saskia. On top of this, Alix soon discovers the feud between her landlady and her neighbours, twins Cameron and Grant. Despite being warned to stay away, Alix is drawn to Cameron's warm nature. With his plans to move north and her turbulent past, could they have a future together?

SILENCED WITNESS

Tracey Walsh

Morven Jennings is a super recogniser: she has the ability to remember the faces of almost everyone she's ever seen. Having lived under an assumed identity in witness protection since the murder of her parents when she was sixteen, she hopes one day to spot the face of the killer in a CCTV image. But when her investigation of the abduction of a baby from Heathrow Airport takes her down unexpected avenues, it brings shadows of her past to light — and puts her in the sights of dangerous enemies . . .